THE LAST CHRISTMAS

Bill Thompson

Published by
Ascendente Books
Dallas, Texas

Published by Ascendente Books
ISBN 978-17355661-1-5
Printed in the United States of America

Books by Bill Thompson

In the fall of 2019, my wife and I joined Judy Lowstuter of Celtic Journeys and several others in Edinburgh. We took a bus tour of the Highlands on a journey called Haunted Scotland. The castle in this book is loosely based on Dunnottar Castle, a fascinating place.

The scenery was some of the most beautiful we've ever seen, and there were friendly people at every stop along the way. We visited castles and stayed in centuries-old inns, we learned a lot about the Jacobites and the Battle of Culloden, and we learned a lot about the man who would be king, Bonnie Prince Charlie.

To Judy, guide Alison, driver Gary and fellow travelers, this one's for you!

CHAPTER ONE

As crackling flames warmed her bedroom, Lady Benevolence Dayne doubted her wisdom once again, perhaps for the hundredth time since she'd posted the letters to her family a week ago.

A grizzled old Scotsman stood some distance away, his Dayne tartan kilt moving lightly back and forth as he floated in the air. "You appreciate the importance of this homecoming," he said. "Why then do you let the decision prey on your mind?"

"I suppose I fear they won't come. It's been so many years..."

"They will, because you gave them great incentive," the man replied. "They'd be fools not to come see what it is you're up to. Will you tell them the tragedy that befell you?"

Benevolence said it would depend on how the visits went. They might depart without ever knowing, she added, but if the time and situation were right, perhaps she would tell them.

"The anniversary of Lord Dayne's death is fast approaching," he said. "Nicholas must do what is right by the clan. If he doesn't...but enough, milady. Good luck to you. Good luck to us both. It's time for rounds. We must keep the Redcoats at bay, you know."

She laughed. "Malcolm, you're an old fool. It's the twenty-first century. There hasn't been a Redcoat in this castle in two hundred years."

"Thanks in no small part to my vigilance." He moved to the heavy oaken door and passed through it easily. Once he was gone, Lady Dayne sat on the edge of the bed and wept. She was enticing four adults and their families — two children of her own and two of her husband's from a previous marriage — to come home against their wills. Three came for their father's funeral nine years ago, but there had been no visits since. A few calls from her stepdaughter Noelle in London marked her only contact with any of them. Her blood children hadn't bothered.

Weeping wasn't becoming, she told herself as she regained her stolid composure and idly arranged the pleats of her long black skirt. A knock came on the door, and Laris, the housekeeper, apologized for intruding but reminded Benevolence it was cocktail hour.

The old woman stood, walked into the ancient castle's wide hallway and down stone stairs to the great room, where Malcolm Dayne sat in a chair by the fire, his favorite single-malt Scotch already in hand.

CHAPTER TWO

NICHOLAS
November 2020
Upper East Side, New York City

"Glad you're home, honey. A letter came for you today. It's from your mother."

"That's interesting." He smiled as he closed the door and dropped his briefcase in the study. "Is it postmarked from Heaven?"

"Okay, okay, not your mother. It's from *her*. You know who I meant."

"Ah, Benevolence, the wicked stepmother. She never calls; she never writes. Wonder what she's up to these days?"

"She'd be up to killing you if she heard you call her the wicked stepmother. Sounds like something from *Grimms' Fairy Tales*."

"Come on, Carly. She lives in a castle in Scotland. I'll bet she offers the children apples." They both chuckled.

Nicholas walked into the kitchen, kissed his wife, and began his ritual. Even if they were going out for the evening, he had his first — and best — martini at home. Hendrick's extra dry straight from the freezer, served in a frozen glass with three blue cheese olives.

She said, "I turned on the patio heaters. Grab a jacket and let's have cocktails outdoors."

Even with the temperature in the forties, their patio was comfortable because it faced away from the stiff north wind. It was Nicholas's favorite place in the evenings, and tonight he stood at the railing, sipped his drink, and marveled once more at the view that made New York special. From the twentieth floor of their Upper East Side apartment, they could see the East River, but the sight that took his breath away lay fifty blocks to the south. The Empire State Building — the symbol of American capitalism — gleamed in the last rays of sunlight. He raised his glass in a toast to life and prosperity as Carly slipped into a chair beside his and handed him the letter.

As he looked at it, he remarked that no one wrote letters these days, so one rarely saw postage stamps. Especially six affixed haphazardly to a brown manila envelope, each one bearing the image of Queen Elizabeth II.

The handwriting was crisp and even, recognizable immediately even after all the years. How long had it been? Nine years since Father passed? He hadn't spoken to Benevolence since he was there for the funeral. As the eldest son and the current earl, he approved the occasional expense for a repair or purchase at the castle, but the family's firm of chartered accountants dealt with him on those things. Nothing involving Torcall Castle or the family required his interaction with his stepmother.

"Are you going to spend the evening reminiscing or open your letter?" Carly teased, and he said he couldn't imagine why she had suddenly decided to write. He tore open the envelope and began to read.

Nicholas, it began. Not "Dear Nicholas," for there was nothing dear between them. *Nicholas, I'm writing to invite you and Carly to Torcall Castle for my last Christmas. It's been many years since you came home to Scotland. Stephanie and Jillian are practically grown-ups now. But I digress. I doubt you think I'm inviting you home because I miss spending Christmas with you, and that's correct. There are important financial matters I must discuss with each of Geoffrey's children, most importantly you, Lord Nicholas Dayne.*

"I know how hard it was for her to write those last three words," he commented. "She never was that keen on me, and now she's living out her remaining years in my house."

He read the rest silently, pausing here and there to consider the nuances of her words. When he finished, he read the entire letter aloud to Carly.

"Comments?" he asked.

"Well, Lord Dayne, it sounds as though we're spending Christmas in Scotland."

CHAPTER THREE

NOELLE
November 2020
The Goose & Gander Pub, Leicester Square, London

"Hey, boss! We're on the last case of Sancerre!"

"Shit!" Noelle had shorted Wednesday's wine order because cash was tight, like always. Now they were low on a bestseller and she'd have to pay extra for a special delivery. She wiped her brow with a bar cloth and fetched drinks for a group of noisy twentysomethings.

Ian emerged from the bottom of the circular staircase that ran up to street level. He called to her from across the room. "Noelle! I'm glad to catch you here. Do you have a moment?"

With a frown and raised eyebrows, Noelle gestured around the crowded pub. "What do you think at half past six on a Friday night in Leicester Square? Did you expect I'd have a moment?" Seeing his face fall, she realized she was taking out her frustration on him. She smiled and said, "Don't despair, darling. I just don't have any time now. See you at midnight." She turned and winced as a server down the bar called out an order for a bottle of Sancerre and six glasses. This was going to be a long evening.

Hours later she rang up the final tab and locked the door behind two lovebirds who lingered until last call. The servers already had the chairs upended on tables and were mopping the floors. They wanted to start their own Friday night celebrations as quickly as possible. Many pubs stayed open until two, and getting off at midnight gave them plenty of time to go partying.

The bartender said, "We're out of Sancerre. Billy's delivering in the morning; shall I order a few cases?"

"Three. If we run out, we run out." She started counting the till, heard a rap at the door, and looked up. There was Ian, and this time she was glad to see him. When he came after closing, it meant an extra set of hands to get her home that much faster.

A few minutes before one they set the alarm system, locked up, and climbed the stairs, emerging into the hubbub of late-night Leicester Square. At Charing Cross Station they caught the tube to Lewisham. They'd be in Greenwich in under an hour and at the flat soon thereafter.

"Was it a good night?" he asked as they took seats on the crowded train.

"Two thousand quid on cards and nearly a thousand in cash," she whispered, patting the backpack where she'd stashed the bank envelope. It was more cash than usual, and if Ian hadn't been along, she'd have made a night deposit at NatWest rather than carrying it home. "Better than normal. Tonight was busy as hell. I'm not sure why, but I'm not complaining."

She picked up the mail as they entered her building. They walked up two flights of stairs and she flopped down on the couch.

"Nightcap?" he asked, and she nodded. "Whisky neat for me. It's been a night, for sure." She glanced through the mail. Bill. Circular. Circular. Bill. And then she came to something different. A brown manila envelope posted from Scotland.

"I'll be damned," she muttered as she opened the letter. "Wonder what the old bird's doing writing to me."

Ian said, "The old bird? Who's that?"

"My stepmother, Benevolence. I haven't heard from her since my father's funeral. That's been, what…eight or nine years, I suppose. Time flies."

Ian handed her the drink. "Benevolence. Who'd hang that name on a kid?"

"She's American — her family's from Pennsylvania. They were Quakers and kept old traditions alive. Trust me, if you ever meet her, Benevolence will be the last word you'd choose to describe my stepmother." She began to read aloud.

Noelle, I'm sure you are surprised to receive this letter. Knowing your penchant for brutal frankness, I'll dispense with the cordial greetings stepmothers often share with families. You must come home for Christmas. Mitchell and Poppy are invited too, and if you have other children, bring them as well. There are important financial matters to discuss, ones better dealt with by your late father but now left to me.

Please be at Torcall Castle in time for cocktails at six p.m. on December 23. If you arrive in Aberdeen, I will arrange a car and driver to bring you and your family to the castle. You may fly first class, and I will reimburse the cost. You may stay until sundown on December 26, Boxing Day. If you wish to remain in the area longer, you may arrange accommodations elsewhere at your expense.

Noelle read the remaining paragraphs silently, folded the letter, and said, "She wants me to go home for Christmas." She knew Ian would complain, but the last paragraphs mentioned money. If there was a chance to get money from her father's second wife, she had to go. It would be an easy overnight trip on the sleeper train from London's Euston Station to Fort William, and then a trip on the steam train to Mallaig.

"A little late for Christmas invites, don't you agree? It's friggin' November already, and we have plans," he said.

"You promised we'd go to Brighton for our first Christmas together."

"Shit happens, Ian. You're forty-seven years old. Get over it. I'm tired and I'm going to bed."

Unable to put the letter out of her mind, Noelle lay awake and thought about her stepmother's words.

Mitchell and Poppy are invited too, Benevolence had said. That's a riot. You're a little behind on your news, stepmother. Mitchell ran off with that tart he worked with at the bank. And I haven't laid eyes on Poppy since I told her I wouldn't give her another penny until she got a job. She dropped out of high school and disappeared. Good riddance.

Now I have Ian, who's eighteen years younger than I, and a busker at Victoria Station. Not much in the ambition department, but good in bed and pleasant company on lonely nights. Maybe I'll take Ian with me. That might be fun.

She dismissed that thought in seconds when she considered how his presence might complicate their relationship. Ian was unaware she came from a seriously wealthy family. How could he know, watching her scrape by every day at the bar? That said, she would never be wealthy herself. She had expected an inheritance, but instead she got a rude awakening. Her father left everything to his firstborn son — her brother, Nicholas — including a lordship. Nicky became the new Earl of Torcall.

What a sardonic load of shit that news had been. Nicky, already fabulously wealthy doing some kind of banking in New York, got the castle and twenty thousand acres to boot. She got the news shortly after her father's funeral. After his service at the village church, everyone had gathered at Torcall Castle, the Dayne ancestral home, and she was mingling with guests in the great room when a man came over and introduced himself.

He was a solicitor with a Glasgow firm the family had used for generations, a man in his sixties who offered condolences over the death of Lord Dayne. She had casually asked if she'd be required to return to Scotland for the reading of her father's will.

"It won't be necessary," the man had said, instantly and unknowingly crushing her lifelong dream of finally having a little money for retirement, the occasional trip, and some excitement in her mundane existence. The man added salt to the wound, saying, "The only heir is your brother Nicholas. As the next earl, he inherits everything. I spoke with him briefly after Lord Dayne's passing. It is his intention to give his siblings twenty thousand pounds each, a generous gesture, in my opinion."

Twenty thousand pounds. What a laugh that had been. Nicky was the only one who had made a success of his life. He was a gazillionaire already, and now he got the castle and twenty thousand acres. She was barely making it as a publican, her sister, Tiona, was doing God knew what in America somewhere, and Aidan — no one had heard from Aidan in years.

She was pissed off at her father for a very long time for doing such a Victorian thing in a world where women's rights mattered. Then she came to grips with the fact that a Scottish earl living in a hundred-room castle on the sea might not view the world as others did. He had passed on the inheritance and the title just as the Earls of Torcall before him. She gave up on blaming him, although he had done her no favors.

Now Benevolence wanted them to come home. All things considered, it was crazy to consider taking Ian, even if her stepmother paid all the expenses. If he saw the place where she grew up, it would change everything between them. Daughter of a Scottish earl and raised in the lap of luxury, he'd think, and she'd never convince him it didn't belong to her. He would think of her as wealthy, and he'd also see the friction that always arose at Dayne family gatherings.

Poppy was a different story. If she could find her daughter, Noelle would insist she come along. The promise of money might entice the girl, although for all Noelle knew, she might be quite well off. She hadn't spoken to Poppy in years, but she still was friends with her on Facebook, and that was how she reached out to the girl.

Yes, she would accompany Noelle. No, she didn't need any help. She could pay her own way just fine, thank you. She would meet her at Euston on December twenty-second for the overnight train ride.

Noelle wasn't certain how she and Poppy would interact after so much time had passed. But one thing was certain; she had no expectations about money this time. Her dreams had been crushed so completely that she could barely think of facing her brother — the Earl of Torcall. But she'd go. She was curious, it was free, and Benevolence had called it the Last Christmas. What the hell did that mean?

CHAPTER FOUR

TIONA
November 2020
Greenwich Village, New York City

As the subway rumbled into the West Fourth Street station, Tiona stood and grabbed the strap, jostling with others as the car swayed back and forth. She detested rush hour, but no matter how much planning she did, she rarely got away from the office before seven. In November, that meant going home on a crowded train in the dark.

She walked past Washington Square, which on a summer evening would be filled with NYU students. On this cold mid-November night, it was empty. The wind whipped newspapers into a mini-tornado as a homeless man on a park bench shifted in his sleeping bag.

He might freeze to death, Tiona thought idly as she remembered tonight's forecast for light snow and thirty degrees. She was shivering by the time she reached her building, unlocked the door, and stepped into the vestibule. She opened her mailbox, tossed ninety percent of it into a waste can full of other people's discards, and saw the manila envelope.

As she rode the elevator, she looked at the familiar golden seal in the upper left corner. Torcall Castle, Inverness-shire, Scotland. The words encircled the Dayne family crest, and she wondered what possessed her mother to write after all this time.

She changed into sweats, poured a glass of wine, and dug out a menu from the Chinese place down the street. She placed an order for delivery, sat at the table, and opened the letter.

Tiona, my daughter. It has been nine years since we spoke, and I regret that you chose silence over communication. You were at university the last I heard, but when you stopped requesting money, I presumed you quit school, just as you have done with everything else important in your life. I hope this address is current; my solicitor found it through a search. I want you to come home for Christmas. If you have a spouse and children, they are welcome as well. Certain financial matters require your attendance, and selfishly, I would appreciate your spending a Christmas with your mother.

She stopped and took a sip of wine, surprised that her mother could still piss her off so easily, even after nine years of silence.

She accuses me of not communicating? Last I knew, the phone line went both ways. And school? I could have graduated if I wanted, but I got a job at Teller Broadcasting. Part time, but then full time with long days and no time for school. Screw you, Mother. I don't need your money anymore. Not that there was ever that much to begin with.

Tiona read on.

Please be at Torcall Castle in time for cocktails at six p.m. on December 23. If you arrive in Glasgow, I will arrange a car and driver to bring you and your family to the castle. You may fly first class, and I will reimburse the cost. You may stay here until December 26, Boxing Day, at six o'clock in the evening. If you wish to remain in the area longer, you may arrange accommodations elsewhere at your expense.

Given the tempestuous relationships between us all, you understand my invitation is not caused by my desire to gather the family at table for a Last Christmas dinner. As I said, there are urgent matters that should not be ignored.

THE LAST CHRISTMAS

She read the remaining paragraph and then read it all again. *Mother's paying for my first-class flight to Scotland. I've never flown first class. It would only be three nights at the castle, since her invitation expires on Boxing Day. She mentions gathering family. I wonder if the others got letters too.*

And there is that last paragraph. The part about money and secrets. She promises to make the visit worth my while.

Tiona last saw her half-siblings at Father's funeral in 2011. Back then, she learned that Nicholas's Manhattan office was only five blocks from hers, but their lives couldn't have been more different. He and his wife, Carly, lived in luxury somewhere on the Upper East Side while she existed in a studio apartment in the Village. He made millions in investment banking while she eked out a living in the social media department at Teller, a cable broadcasting network.

Benevolence Dayne's other child, her blood brother, Aidan, was another story. She hadn't seen him in, what — twelve years? If it weren't for him, she'd have been her mother's biggest disappointment. But Aidan was the black sheep of the herd.

After reading the letter, Tiona had no choice but to go. Benevolence was dangling a carrot she couldn't resist. Tonight she'd go online and book a flight, and six weeks from now she'd be in Scotland, for better or for worse.

CHAPTER FIVE

AIDAN
December 2020
Sangre de Cristo Mountains, New Mexico

The last embers of the campfire emitted a pulsing glow as the couple snuggled into the sleeping bag. The dawn would bring snow, but inside the tent it was cozy and warm.

"I like you a whole lot, Aidan Dayne," she said, giving him a peck on the cheek. "Wish it were warmer so we could take our clothes off. Not tonight, though. We don't want to freeze off anything important of yours."

He laughed and pulled her close. "You're something else, Isabella. Two misfits, one twice as old as the other. How on earth did we get together?"

"Dunno, baby. I hoped to find Prince Charming. I guess I got him, minus the castle."

Yet I was born in one, he thought to himself. *There's so much this girl doesn't know about me, but I've only known her two weeks. Someday maybe I'll tell her more, but right now it's too early.*

They slept until the trill of songbirds in the tall pines woke them. Aidan tugged on his waterproof coat and pants and crawled out into an inch of snow. He'd prepared everything last night, and within minutes coffee bubbled on the Coleman stove. The dry wood he had stacked under a small tarp caught quickly, and soon a great fire crackled and popped.

It was a frigid December morning in central New Mexico. Majestic snowcapped peaks of the Sangre de Cristo mountains surrounded their campsite. The air was icy and fresh and the sky cloudless as Aidan sat by the campfire, enjoying the spectacular scene.

He heard Isabella stir in the tent. "Damn, it's cold!"

"Better bundle up. It's freezing out here too, but God, it's beautiful."

They clinked coffee mugs, watched a doe and her fawn pass within twenty feet of them, and saw a bald eagle soaring lazily in the winter sky. They took a hike into the dense forest, and then he fixed bacon and eggs on the stove.

"There's something special about having breakfast out in the wild," he said, and she agreed. Isabella hadn't spent the night outdoors before, but she said she loved it. Aidan did this often and had all the right equipment, which made winter camping not just tolerable, but fun.

What she didn't know was that in the years since he came to America, this tent had often been his home. He stayed in a trailer at the moment, but he would be happy when the day came that he lived in these mountains again.

They prepared to leave, packing the gear in the bed of his old pickup, picking up trash, and dousing the campfire. On the way back, they talked about Christmas. It was six days away, and she said she might go to Colorado to see her parents.

"Or I might spend it with you," she added, fishing for an invitation, but Aidan didn't bite. Christmas was never a fun holiday for him, and this year would be worse since he could hardly pay his bills, much less buy her a present. They barely knew each other, and he looked forward to spending another Christmas alone.

"I have plans," he snapped, his words harsher than he intended, and she said nothing for the remainder of the trip.

When he arrived at her apartment complex in Santa Fe, she got out, grabbed her backpack, slammed the car door, and walked away without so much as a wave.

As he drove I-20 south to Rosario, he doubted he'd see Isabella again. He'd pissed off another one, but he really didn't care. It wasn't all his fault — Izzy was hotheaded and petulant a lot of the time. Relationships were for other people. Aidan Dayne was a loner and didn't mind it a bit.

He drove into the RV park, waved at his neighbors, and parked in front of a rusting double-wide he rented for forty bucks a week. He unloaded the equipment, took things inside that needed washing, and checked his watch. He had to be at work in two hours.

As he stepped out of the shower, someone knocked at the door. "One sec," he yelled, pulling on sweatpants.

A mail carrier asked his name and handed him a crumpled, dirty manila envelope with lots of scribbling on it. The stamps were from Great Britain.

"This one's been around the block. Came from Scotland, according to the postmark," the mailman said. "Looks like the postal service forwarded it more than once. Have you lived here long?"

"Apparently not long enough," Aidan replied. "Just a few weeks. I'm surprised it found me."

He saw the golden seal of Torcall Castle in the left corner and recognized the handwriting on the envelope. His mother had sent it to Denver, where someone marked out the address and put his next one, which was Taos, but he hadn't lived there since ski season last winter. The last girl he dated must have received the letter and sent it here, because no one else from his past knew where he was.

If it weren't for her, I'd never have seen this letter. Would that have been a good thing or a bad one? Only by opening it would he know the answer.

Aidan, my son. I hope you are well and surviving, and I regret that you missed your father's funeral nine years ago, but from what I heard about your situation, it came as no surprise. I am sending this letter to your last known address in hopes you receive it. You must come home for Christmas. If you have a spouse and children, bring them along. There are important financial matters that require your presence, or else I would not have asked. You might even enjoy spending Christmas at home, as other children seem to do.

Please arrive at Torcall Castle in time for cocktails at six p.m. on December 23. If you arrive in Glasgow, I will arrange a car and driver to bring you and your family to the castle. You may fly first class, and I will reimburse the cost. You may stay here until December 26, Boxing Day, at six p.m. If you wish to remain in the area longer, you may arrange accommodations elsewhere at your expense.

Given the tempestuous relationships between us all, you understand my invitation is not caused by my desire to gather the family at table for a Last Christmas dinner. As I said, there are urgent matters that should not be ignored.

I will make your visit worthwhile. Since money drives all of Geoffrey Dayne's offspring, money is what I promise in exchange for your spending Christmas with me in your childhood home. Money and answers you should have been given long ago. Secrets of your family's past.

Send your travel details to the family solicitor, whose contact information appears below.

Benevolence Dayne

He wadded up the letter and threw it across the room. Her remark about how he might enjoy Christmas like other children was typical, and she signed it with her full name.

Could you have written "Mother," Mother? Like other parents do?

There were many reasons for ignoring her summons. First among those was the timing — her letter was postmarked in early November, but with all the forwarding, it had arrived only three days before he was required to be at

Torcall Castle. He'd signed on to work long hours at the casino through the holidays. Everyone else wanted time off for Christmas with family, and he would get time and a half for the holidays plus overtime if he wanted it. The tables would be packed day and night, and Aidan had mentally banked the thousands of dollars he'd be earning.

Mother promised to reimburse his travel expenses, but he had forty-two dollars in the bank, hardly enough to buy a plane ticket to Europe. Then there was the thought of seeing her, listening to her condescending words about what a mess he'd made of his life, and enduring the incessant nagging about getting an education and a "real" job. Finally there was her odd comment about gathering family for a last Christmas dinner. He had no love for his stepsiblings and wasn't that crazy about his blood sister, Tiona, either. But a "last" dinner? What the hell was she talking about?

Aidan had all the right reasons for staying in New Mexico. And only one reason for going. He picked up the letter, smoothed it out, and read the next-to-last paragraph again. Despite Aidan's situation, his family was wealthy. His father had been an earl, for God's sake, and Torcall Castle sat on umpteen thousand acres of land near Mallaig on Scotland's west coast.

Mother mentioned money. Answers too, but answers weren't important. Money was something else entirely.

How could I make this work? That evening as he worked the blackjack table at the Golden Valley Casino, he considered various possibilities. By the time his shift ended, he had an idea.

CHAPTER SIX

December 22

The British Airways first-class lounge at JFK was more crowded than Nicholas had expected this close to the holidays. At the entrance stood an enormous Christmas tree with dozens of gaily wrapped empty boxes beneath, and soft carols played throughout the club. Like many other New York executives, Nicholas used the lounge often. Tonight well-heeled holiday revelers heading to Europe for Christmas filled almost every seat.

"Welcome back, Lord Dayne," the desk attendant said. "It's chockablock tonight, but you'll find room, I'm sure. Paper boarding passes, or will you be using the app on your phone?"

He opted for paper, and she printed four passes. He directed his family to a table in the bar, where the girls sat and pulled out their AirPods and tablets. A server greeted Nicholas by name and took their orders.

He saw his wife, Carly, studying the room, and asked what she was doing.

"I'm looking for Tiona. She lives in the City, right? Doesn't she work for Teller Broadcasting? I figured she'd be on this flight, since we all have to be in Scotland by tomorrow evening."

"I doubt Tiona knows that first-class lounges exist," he snorted, but had to eat his words moments later when she entered the bar, pulling a wheeled suitcase. Carly waved, and Nicholas said, "What did you do that for? She might not have noticed us."

"Come on, Nicky. She's family. You're cynical about your siblings, but it's Christmas and you're going home. How about a little compassion?"

"She's my half-sister, not my family," he muttered as he rose and gave Tiona a half-hearted hug. He gestured to a chair and asked her to join them. Stephanie and Jillian removed their earbuds just long enough to say hello to the aunt they'd met only once, at Geoffrey Dayne's funeral nine years ago.

Tiona ordered a Bud Light and commented, "This is a nice place. I've never been here. Have you?"

Carly laughed as Nicholas said, "Now and then. To tell the truth, I'm here often. I spend half my time in our London office, and the club makes the airport experience less tedious."

"The servers here see him more than I do," his wife quipped, slapping him on the arm.

Tiona said, "Do you think Mother really will reimburse us for the plane ticket? If she doesn't, my ass is in huge trouble. I borrowed from my 401k to buy a seven-thousand-dollar plane ticket."

He said Benevolence would keep her word, and Tiona drank her beer, calculating how Nicholas had shelled out almost thirty thousand for his family's four tickets. And he did this all the time.

Must be nice.

"What are you doing these days?" Carly asked, and Tiona said she was in the social media department at Teller Broadcasting, a cable news outlet on Sixth Avenue.

"Remind me," Nicholas said. "Is your degree in journalism?"

Some people never change. Twenty-one years older than she, her stepbrother had always treated her like a

26

second-class citizen. "You know I didn't graduate," she replied.

"I didn't know you ever enrolled." She let that one go; he was right, but they were facing four days together and the flight home. It wasn't worth starting things this early.

She changed the subject. "Carly, have you heard if Noelle's coming?"

"We haven't, although if she still lives in London, it would be an easy trip for her. What about your brother? What's he up to?"

Tiona doubted any of them would find this trip easy. She said she hadn't heard from Aidan since long before her father's funeral. She didn't know where he was these days, and unless her mother found him somehow, she doubted Aidan received a letter.

Nicholas tended to a few last-minute business items on his laptop while Tiona and Carly chatted about why Benevolence had sent the cryptic invitation. To Tiona's knowledge, none of Geoffrey Dayne's four children had returned to Scotland since his funeral in 2011, although as heir and the newest earl, Nicholas communicated regularly with the family solicitors and chartered accountants.

The old man's will had come as a surprise to everyone. First came the revelation that Nicholas, who was already a wealthy investment banker, won the jackpot. She couldn't help resenting her father's decision — and hating Nicholas too — but there was no use wasting energy over it.

Lord Dayne gave Nicky Torcall Castle and twenty thousand acres of land, but he left everything else — priceless possessions inside the castle and on its vast grounds — to his second wife, Benevolence. And now it was she who summoned the family for the "last" Christmas — whatever that meant — and promised to dole out money and secrets to those who attended.

Tiona looked for Aidan at the departure gate, all the while knowing he wouldn't be there. As they boarded, she watched Nicholas's girls easily settle into their sumptuous pods, complete with lie-flat beds and TV screens. She observed how familiar with this lifestyle they were, as she gave up and asked a flight attendant where her seat was.

She looked through the amenity kit on the table beside her seat and took out a pair of comfy slippers. In another bag she found pajamas, a soft duvet and a fluffy pillow. *Damn, a person could get used to this if they had a shitload of money*, she thought as she put them aside for later.

"Would you care for a drink before takeoff, Miss Dayne?" the attendant asked, and she ordered a mimosa. She glanced across the aisle into Stephanie's pod and saw her thumbing through the movie selections on her personal screen. Maybe she'd watch a movie too. She didn't want to fall asleep and miss the experience, because unless there was a miracle, she'd never fly first class again once this trip was over.

The Airbus pushed back from the gate on time, rose into the air, and crossed Manhattan island before turning north. The rare times she had flown over the city, Tiona marveled at the sheer beauty of a thousand tall buildings and a million twinkling lights. She saw the new World Trade Center, the tallest building in the country, its sleek spire rising toward the sky. And out in the harbor stood the Statue of Liberty, its gleaming lamp piercing the twilight.

The flight attendant helped Tiona adjust her seat and began bringing things to eat and drink. There was a bowl of mixed nuts so tasty she accepted a refill. And another mimosa, after which she switched to some French white wine that tasted wonderful.

She dozed off, awakening when someone touched her shoulder. A flight attendant handed her a little white egg-roll thingy that turned out to be a piping hot towel for her hands, and another person handed her a menu. Damn if they didn't have a selection of items for dinner!

She ordered a steak — a rare treat for a salaried girl living in an expensive town — and when it came, the server suggested she switch to a red wine to accompany the meat. *Of course she did. We don't want to be having white wine when the other people in first class are having red with their steaks, right?*

Nicholas stopped by after dinner and asked if she needed anything. No, she told him, and she snuggled down into the duvet, chose *The Marvelous Mrs. Maisel*, fixed her pillow just right, and within minutes she was sound asleep.

"Miss? Miss, it's time to wake up." She grumbled and turned away, but whoever it was seemed insistent. Uncertain of her whereabouts, she opened her eyes and saw the flight attendant smiling at her. "We'll be landing in an hour, and we're starting our breakfast service. Would you care to start with a coffee or some tea?"

Damn, I could get accustomed to this, she mused as she ordered coffee, stretched and yawned, put on her comfy slippers, and plodded to the first-class bathroom that was larger than the one in her apartment.

CHAPTER SEVEN

December 23

The plane landed at Heathrow at just past six in the morning. Tiona walked off the plane with Nicholas and his family, watching as a British Airways representative greeted him and ushered his family into a cart bearing the airline's logo. Knowing it wasn't meant for her, she pulled her rolling suitcase down the hallway.

Carly called out, "Tiona, come with us," and she climbed aboard.

As the cart whisked them through a maze of long, narrow hallways in the bowels of the massive airport, they passed hundreds of people toting heavy suitcases and crying children. Tiona hadn't experienced the amenities that wealth brought to the travel experience, and she told herself it would be easy to get used to this.

As they exited customs, Nicholas insisted she check her suitcase for the short flight to Scotland rather than dealing with it. After taking a bus ride to the domestic terminal, Nicholas led them to another comfortable airline lounge. Three hours later they arrived in Glasgow.

Tiona wondered who would meet them here. As they exited the secure area with their luggage, she spied a man wearing a cap and holding a white card with their family crest emblazoned on it. She pointed him out to Nicholas, who caught the man's eye.

"May I presume you are Lord Dayne?" the young man asked, and Nicholas nodded. "Welcome to Scotland, all of you! I'm John, your mother's handyman."

"Thank you for meeting us," Nicholas said. "You're new. How long have you been at the castle?"

"Two years. Lady Dayne hired the wife and me, and after Barclay…uh, became too old to drive, I added chauffeur to my job description."

There was rain and a biting wind, and John situated them under a canopy while he brought the car around. Others waiting for rides stared as a 1955 Rolls-Royce Silver Wraith pulled to the curb, and John held the door for the family. He stowed the luggage in the boot and pulled away, the car's wipers struggling to keep up with the rainstorm.

As they drove through rolling meadows and hills with crests hidden by dense, low-hanging clouds, Tiona thought about Barclay, her father's chauffeur. As a child she had loved going into the garage, where sat three Rolls-Royces, one a convertible. Every time she came, she found him working on them. If he wasn't tinkering under the hood, he was polishing headlights with a cloth. She loved the man because unlike her parents, he always had time for her. He allowed her to talk, asked her opinion about things, and listened to her answers.

"Is Barclay still with Mother?" Tiona asked, and John said yes, he was there but had limited responsibilities these days. She learned that Mrs. Keith — whom everyone called Cook — and Mrs. Campbell, the housekeeper, were still there as well. All three had been servants in the household when they were children, and she wondered how old they must be by now. She figured young John and his wife did most of the work around the castle nowadays.

"Are we the first to arrive?" Nicholas asked, and John nodded. He would pick up Noelle at the train station in Mallaig soon after dropping them at the castle. Tiona asked about Aidan, but the chauffeur hadn't heard about another arrival.

They turned off the main highway onto a country lane lined with white wooden fences. Sheep grazed in the meadows, picking at what grass they could find at this time of year, and Carly remarked how nice it felt to be back on the Dayne estate at last.

"I'll reserve my judgment until I see how Benevolence acts," Nicholas commented. Carly shushed him so John wouldn't hear, but it was too late, and the driver had the same thought. Why had Benevolence summoned them? Given the situation at Torcall Castle, she took a dangerous risk allowing outsiders — especially family — inside the walls. What if?…but he stopped himself. She had some reason for doing this foolish thing, and it wasn't his place to question her reasons.

CHAPTER EIGHT

"The first look at our home always takes my breath away," Tiona whispered as the Rolls drew near the ancient structure. Torcall Castle had stood on a craggy hill overlooking the ocean since 1452. Generations of the clan Dayne had lived within its walls, served their kings, and fought bloody battles for Scotland's independence.

Today the bulk of the two-hundred-room castle lay in ruins. Patches of grass sprang from the once-impenetrable rock walls that long ago enclosed dining halls, stables and kitchens. The ruins stood as silent reminders of the days when knights and royals — even the Queen herself — walked those grand halls as guests of the laird and his lady.

John pulled the Rolls to the front of the west tower, the still-standing one that held almost a hundred rooms, only twenty in use today. In a scene reminiscent of *Downton Abbey*, a small contingent of servants stood at attention in the driveway, umbrellas raised against the sprinkles of rain. Nicholas remarked on how different things were. Three people awaited their arrival instead of the fourteen who served his father and mother when he was a child. There were the familiar faces of Mrs. Campbell and Barclay and Cook. It surprised him how little they seemed to have changed in nine years. He was sixty-seven and they had to be twenty years older, but they somehow looked even younger than when he last came.

The castle's enormous front door opened, and Benevolence Dayne walked out and down the sidewalk toward them like a movie star on the red carpet. She held the arm of a maid — perhaps John's wife — who walked alongside and shielded her with an umbrella.

"Mother's typical grand entrance," Tiona snipped as John helped the girls out of the Rolls and unpacked the luggage. Stephanie and Jillian had been nine and six when they came for the funeral. Back then, they'd compared Torcall Castle to something from Disney, and now as teenagers, it seemed even more imposing, majestic and forbidding as the dark clouds framed its ruined towers.

"Hello, Benevolence," Nicholas said, giving her their usual air kiss. The lack of warmth always surprised his wife, Carly, who knew she'd get only a handshake. Tiona — Benevolence's blood child — got a tiny hug, but nothing more.

I'll bet she practiced that hug all morning. Carly chided herself for such a catty thought as they greeted the elderly servants. Cook — whom no one called by her actual name, which was Mrs. Keith — and Mrs. Campbell, the housekeeper, had served the family for decades. Barclay too — he had been Lord Dayne's valet and chauffeur back in the day. John introduced everyone to his wife, Laris, who was now Lady Dayne's housemaid.

"The staff will attend to your luggage," Benevolence said. "Come in out of the damp. There's a pleasant fire in the great room." As they followed her down the hall, John said as soon as he finished with the luggage, he would head to Mallaig to meet Noelle's train.

Laris wheeled in a trolley laden with a bucket of ice, bottles of gin, vodka, red and white wine, and a variety of mixers. Nicholas made a show of looking at his watch. "Drinks before noon, Stepmother? What would Father say?"

"He would say it's Christmastime, and the family has come home. That calls for a drink."

THE LAST CHRISTMAS

Carly had watched Tiona fidget all morning, and she chalked it up to anxiety over seeing her mother again. God knew the old woman made her nervous too. She watched Tiona sit, then stand, then move around the room, picking out a book here, examining a framed photograph there. It was as if she couldn't be still. In a moment she asked to be excused, saying she needed to freshen up.

Benevolence rang a little silver bell that sat on a table by her chair, and Mrs. Campbell's quick entrance made Carly wonder if she'd been listening just outside the room. No, she decided. Most likely, her mother-in-law's impatience caused the staff to stay close by.

"Take Tiona upstairs to her bedroom," Lady Dayne said, but Tiona shook her head.

"I think I can find my old bedroom by myself." She went to the grand staircase and climbed to the second floor. Bursting into her room and slamming the door behind her, she saw her suitcase lying open on a bench and ran to it.

Tiona ignored her surroundings and focused on just one thing — relief. Her hands shook as she dug through the bag to a zippered pocket in the side. She removed a plastic bag, took out a brown bottle, and popped two Xanax tablets in her mouth. Then she returned the bag to its compartment.

She lay on the bed with her eyes closed as a sense of peace spread through her body. Her panic assuaged by the pills, she inhaled deeply as she lay in the room that once was her own. She'd left the castle at age seventeen in a rebellious huff, moved to America to be far from her domineering parents, and when she returned nine years ago for her father's funeral, she learned she no longer had claim to her old sanctuary. Benevolence had removed every semblance of Tiona's life and personality and turned it into a guest room. It had saddened her then to see the room once filled with her memories as a sterile, lifeless place.

Calm enough now to rejoin the family, Tiona opened her eyes and looked around the room for the first time.

Above her hung a colorful light fixture decorated with Disney characters. She'd gotten it for her fifth birthday and loved it so much that even as a teenager she never replaced it. She saw Mickey and Goofy and Cinderella...her childhood friends.

How can this be? The Disney chandelier wasn't here last time.

She felt goosebumps on her arms, and she abruptly sat up. *How can this be? Who made this happen...and why?*

Nine years ago — the last time she came to Torcall Castle — the Disney chandelier had been gone. In its place hung a modern stainless steel contraption with six arms. But there hung the fixture from her childhood. As she took in more of the room, she realized everything was back to the old days.

The room was hers again, completely restored to a time before she left in 1998. Stuffed animals lay on her chair and bed, and the iPhone 4 she got for her twelfth birthday sat exactly where she left it. She ran to her closet and opened the door. Tacked inside was the Lady Gaga poster her father wouldn't allow her to hang on the bedroom wall. Clothes — *her* clothes from her teenage years — hung in rows in the closet. Clothes that hadn't been here nine years ago.

She shivered as she remembered something. A little afraid of what she might find, she removed a corner tack from the concert poster and pulled it back. She looked at the words scrawled on the door with a marking pen.

I love Benjamin Nuttall.

Holy shit. She ran her fingers over the words. *Holy shit. I wrote that when I was thirteen years old.* When she came nine years ago, this door had been repainted a stark white and the inscription was gone. Today the wood was the same old faded beige, nicked with the wear and tear inflicted by a child. And the words — thirty-three-year-old words — were in her handwriting.

Her hands trembled as she considered what this meant. For a moment she had believed her mother restored the room for some bizarre reason. But that wasn't possible. Where would she have stored everything? How would she have returned things to their exact places from long ago? And how does one make a newly painted door old again? How do you recreate your thirteen-year-old daughter's handwriting…and why?

No, this was about something else. She didn't believe in time warps or parallel dimensions, but as she stood in the ancient castle where she grew up, nothing seemed too far-fetched to consider.

Before returning to the others, she walked across the hall to Nicholas's bedroom. He had been off at university when she was born, and he'd moved to America when she was four. Tiona still remembered the day her mother and the servants removed all his things too. She wanted to see what had changed in there, but before she reached the door, she heard noise from the floor below — a brash voice that was annoying even after nine years had passed. Her half-sister, Noelle, had arrived. She stuck her head through the doorway, took a quick look around Nicky's bedroom, and went downstairs.

Of Geoffrey Dayne's four children, only Noelle Dayne Curzon could be called gregarious, although it was a lie. Noelle was one of those who arrived at every function late so she could make an entrance. Tiona knew why; all of the Dayne children had self-esteem issues, but as adults Nicholas and Noelle hid theirs behind façades. Nicky's was a warmth that wasn't heartfelt. Noelle masked her insecurities by a false cordiality.

"Darling," Noelle cooed as Tiona entered the room. She tossed about air kisses and hugs like balloons in the air, and she took the floor with an exhausting story about how dull the train ride from London had been.

"When you've seen one flock of sheep on the hills, you've seen 'em all." She sighed dramatically. "I'd forgotten how damn many sheep there are up here. It's a shame we don't eat mutton all the time like the Brits!"

Shaken from her experience in the bedroom, Tiona wanted to tell Nicky about it, but with Noelle's arrival, she figured she might as well give her sister some attention and get it over with. She asked, "Did Poppy come with you? I haven't seen her in ages. She missed the funeral, if I recall correctly."

Noelle turned beet red. "What a keen memory you have, Tiona. Yes, she missed the funeral, but she came along this time. Nicky's daughters grabbed her the moment we got inside the castle. They've gone off somewhere."

Benevolence said, "I'm sure she came because she thought her grandmother was going to pass out fifty-pound notes like Christmas candy."

Noelle was losing it fast. "Listen, Benevolence, I don't know why she came. I read your letter to her, and she agreed to accompany me. Can we leave it at that?"

Tiona broke the icy chill by changing the subject. "Mother, what do you hear from Aidan?"

Benevolence sniffed. "Nothing, just as I expected. And frankly, even your coming surprised me. It's a long trip for someone in your…"

Tiona bristled. "My *what*, Mother? My financial circumstances? I'll admit I don't have money like Nicholas and Noelle, but I came because I wanted to see you."

Noelle smiled. She barely had tuppence to rub together, but that was her secret. As far as they knew, she was a successful London publican.

"My dear, like the others, you came because I told you there would be money in it for you. None of you have darkened my door since your father's funeral nine years ago. Nicholas and Noelle, I can understand. They're stepchildren to me. But my blood children — you, and especially Aidan

— disappoint me. He left home a year after you did. Just packed his things and walked out one day. I suppose he couldn't stomach being in the castle alone with his mother. He never even said goodbye."

CHAPTER NINE

Breaking a period of uncomfortable silence, Benevolence rang the bell to summon Mrs. Campbell, informing her they were ready to be seated for lunch. They filed into an enormous dining room half the length of a football field that had forty-foot ceilings. The somber portraits of Daynes throughout the centuries stared down at them from the walls. At the end above the laird's chair hung a life-sized portrait of Bonnie Prince Charlie, who hid at the castle before fleeing for France in 1746 after the Battle of Culloden.

Although the table could accommodate sixty, today eight places were set under the watchful eye of the Stuart prince. Forty feet away at the opposite end stood a tall-backed carved wooden chair and another place setting. When the grandchildren asked about it, Noelle explained that chair was reserved for the famous clan chief Malcolm Dayne, who fought in the Battle of Culloden in April of 1746. To honor his service, his place was set at the table for every meal served in this room.

Tiona touched Nicholas's arm and whispered in his ear about the bedrooms. He nodded and said, "We'll talk after lunch."

Benevolence instructed Nicholas to take his rightful place in the laird's chair at the near end of the table, and she sat to his right. As the others chose seats, the three granddaughters selected chairs as far as possible from the others. They weren't adolescents, with the youngest sixteen and the oldest twenty-three, but they giggled like schoolgirls at something on an iPad.

Benevolence gestured toward them. "Nicholas and Noelle, will you speak to your children, or shall I?"

Nicholas said, "Girls, AirPods out and iPads off the table. That's not appropriate here."

They protested but did as they were told, and Benevolence advised Mrs. Campbell they were ready. She and Cook served the meal while Laris poured wine. The copious amount of food served at Dayne family meals was almost laughable. Tiona often ate a salad at her desk for lunch; Noelle nibbled on a bit of this, a bit of that from the kitchen as the cooks turned out plates for her pub customers; and even Nicholas, who power lunched often, was careful not to overdo the calories.

The food arrived in courses. First came a duck pate with cornichons and capers, then a generous helping of roast beef, haggis and boiled vegetables, followed by a green salad and a sugary sweet Tablet for dessert. There was enough food for an army, Noelle commented, but her stepmother pretended not to hear her.

Although uncomfortable with idle conversation, Benevolence attempted to engage her granddaughters. "Are you girls enjoying yourselves so far? This is only your second visit, and when you came nine years ago, it was only for two nights. The castle has lots of rooms to explore and history to learn, if you'll only put down those machines and venture about."

"How come you didn't decorate for Christmas?" Jillian said. "It feels like Halloween in this creepy old place. Maybe a wreath or some holly would have cheered things up."

"Sorry, Benevolence," Nicholas interjected. "Jill can sometimes speak her mind without thinking." He glared at his daughter, who broke into a fit of giggles that her grandmother snorted was unbecoming for a sixteen-year-old.

Poppy said, "Mom, didn't you tell me there's a village on the estate that's only a mile or two from the castle? I want to go there this afternoon and look around. Anyone want to join me?"

Benevolence raised her voice. "You may not leave the castle. I forbid you to visit the village."

Everyone shifted nervously and wondered why the outburst. Nicholas asked, "What's wrong with them going? It's a beautiful walk along the coast, and they might enjoy seeing the Christmas tree, especially since our family pays to put it in the square every year. Nothing's going to happen to them…"

"I absolutely forbid it. Each of you is here for the money, so you must abide by my rules if you are to get what you came for. Besides, I have something planned for this afternoon."

After an hour of silence pierced by whispered mutterings, the meal was mercifully over. As Benevolence rose from her chair, the others did the same.

"Let's return to the great room," she said. "I have something to tell you."

"May we be excused?" Stephanie asked. Benevolence told them to go do whatever they wanted, and the granddaughters grabbed their earbuds and tablets and fled.

CHAPTER TEN

As everyone seated themselves, Benevolence walked to an antique secretary desk in a corner and picked up a leather portfolio. She returned to her chair, opened the portfolio, and said, "You're going to play a game. For reasons that will become obvious, it's best that each of you competes against the others. With Aidan gone, it will be three of you, each searching for something."

Noelle shook her head. "I'm not much into competitions, Benevolence. Parlor games either. Thanks anyway, but I'll sit this one out."

"None of you was a team player," the woman smirked. "But sitting this one out isn't an option. You may work together if you choose. In fact, joining forces might be safer, because aspects of this game might prove dangerous. There could be pitfalls better handled by a team. But each of you might opt to go it alone once I reveal the goal you're seeking."

She unfolded a piece of paper and said, "I am going to read a series of clues. Commit them to memory; I will read them only once, and you may not write while I am speaking. Are you ready?"

Nicholas said to his siblings, "I'll memorize the first thing she says. When I point to one of you, memorize the next until she's finished. That way we can collaborate."

Their mother smiled. "Collaboration among my children. What a rarity. But yes, you may do as Nicholas suggested."

She began reading.

I watched each of you grow, although I held my tongue about what I saw.

Numbers are very important to me.

I am older than anyone living today.

I have seen wars, rebellions, royalty and treasure.

Although I often communicated, I never spoke.

Mary and Charles are names of great significance.

I hold a secret of immense value.

Who or what am I?

Benevolence put the paper down and watched them repeating their assigned lines aloud so as not to forget them. Nicholas suggested writing them down while they were fresh. Benevolence hadn't allowed it as she read the clues, but now she said nothing.

Everyone wrote furiously except Tiona, who said, "Pardon my French, Mother, but this is a load of crap. I won't be part of some stupid, childish scavenger hunt. Have at it, everyone, but count me out."

"A million pounds sterling. Perhaps more."

Tiona's head popped up. "I beg your pardon?"

"That's what's at stake here. Now is a 'stupid childish scavenger hunt' worth your time?"

Noelle asked, "Are you saying whoever figures out the riddle gets a million quid? What about the losers? When you invited us, you said there was money in it for everyone."

"And there is, my avaricious stepdaughter. The four of you, Aidan included, will receive twenty thousand pounds. That is your inheritance from me, which I will give you on the day after Christmas. That is all you may expect from me."

"Nicky here couldn't care less," Tiona said. "He's the laird. He already inherited everything."

Nicholas winced. Her statement was correct, but not being heirs, his siblings hadn't seen their father's will. True, Nicky was the eighth Earl of Torcall and inherited "everything," but it wasn't as simple as that.

"It takes a fortune to keep this castle and twenty thousand acres going," he said. "True, Father left the property to me, but our chartered accountants in Glasgow administer the funds for maintenance and operations. They collect the rents, pay the bills. The castle costs far more to run than the income it generates. Father's estate makes up the difference."

Tiona didn't believe him. "The entire village of Torcall sits on the Dayne estate, and now it belongs to you. Every business and household pays rent to the laird. Don't bullshit us…"

"You will not use that foul language in this house!" Benevolence shouted, which caused a coughing spasm that lasted more than a minute.

"Sorry, Mother," Tiona muttered.

Nicholas smiled. "Tiona, you always spoke before thinking. You're right, of course. The entire village pays rent. But have you considered the costs of running a fifteenth-century castle, half of which is in ruins? What remains are a hundred drafty rooms, only twenty of them habitable, with a thousand unique problems. I've considered opening it to the public for tours —"

Benevolence interrupted. "But you can't, can you, Nicholas? Your father's will prohibits such intrusions for ten years after his death. Nicholas is the owner of an albatross. It's likely he could use the money as much as the rest of you, but he may or may not end up winning the game. Now, are there any questions?"

Aware of the stipulations in his father's will, Nicholas asked his mother where the million pounds that she just mentioned came from. Geoffrey Dayne had left just thirty thousand pounds a year for his wife's maintenance and well-being, hardly a fortune these days. There had been no mention of an extra million pounds sterling, over one and a quarter million dollars.

She gave a cryptic answer. "It's neither my money nor your father's, nor is it necessarily money at all. Perhaps it is something of even greater worth. You will understand when the riddle is solved."

"Who wrote these clues?" Tiona asked, and Benevolence said their father penned them a few months before his death. "He considered it a way to bring you together as a family. I decided this Christmas — the last Christmas — was the perfect time to unveil your father's handiwork."

"So Father knew what we're looking for?"

"No. He knew only enough to write the clues. He never laid eyes on the prize one of you may discover. Now children, the clock is ticking. Your invitation to Torcall Castle expires at sundown on Boxing Day. That gives you three and a half days to decipher the clues and learn the answer, not counting Christmas Eve morning, when we all must gather to trim the tree, as the family has always done."

"Since you mentioned it, what's so special about everyone leaving on Boxing Day?" Nicholas asked.

"This is my last Christmas, as my letter said. This is the last time you and I will be together. There is a reason why you must be gone by sundown on Boxing Day. Perhaps you will learn it, perhaps not. Leave it at that."

"Mother, how can you say it's your last Christmas?" Tiona asked. "All things in God's time, or so the believers claim."

"This has nothing to do with God. None of you care about the details, nor do I care to share them. So we'll leave it at that. One last thing. Don't forget old Uncle Malcolm. Perhaps he can help with your quest." She laughed, said she was going upstairs to rest, and asked them to join her back in the great room for cocktails at five.

They all rose when Benevolence left. They might not love each other as other families did, but manners and etiquette had been drilled into each of them from infancy. Nannies, tutors and servants taught them how refined Scots acted, and they still remembered.

Nicholas said, "How do we do this? I'm a little old for party games, but I suppose it won't hurt to indulge Benevolence. Something's got her thinking she's on her deathbed."

"She looks healthy as a horse," Noelle commented. "What if this isn't about her health at all? What if it's about something else? And why all the secrets, for God's sake?"

Tiona said, "Because none of us cared enough to communicate with her after Father died. I've meant to call a hundred times and didn't. Having no cellphone, no computer and a landline that only works in nice weather, she's not the easiest person to contact. For nine years, we've all forgotten about her. At least I did." Then she remembered her bedroom. "I need to share something with you. Something very odd is going on in this house."

"Hold on, Tiona. Let's settle the game first," Nicholas said. "Is everyone going to play? It appears there's an opportunity to go home with a million pounds."

Tiona and Noelle nodded.

"All right then, how shall we approach this? Individually or collectively?"

Noelle said, "I vote for individually. These days a million quid isn't that much money. Nicholas, you're rich already, and you inherited the estate. I'm not, and I could use the money. I say we go it alone."

Tiona disagreed. "If we act as a team and I get a third, that's three hundred thousand pounds, which would be a life-changer for me. If we go it alone and work against each other, the losers get only twenty thousand pounds. Carly and the girls can't help you two, because that wouldn't be fair to me. But as a team, there are seven of us. We can do seven times as many things together as one could do alone."

Nicholas agreed, leaving Noelle no choice but to change her mind. "Mother was kidding about our talking to Uncle Malcolm, right?" she asked. "If not, she's gone completely bonkers."

The children knew the Dayne clan's history well. Their bedtime stories hadn't involved pirates and fairies. Instead, they heard about bloody battles for Scotland's sovereignty and heroes like their ancestor Malcolm Dayne and his close friend Bonnie Prince Charlie. There was even a treasure story, a tale of a fortune in Jacobite gold hidden somewhere in the Highlands when Charles fled Scotland. The tales were scary — English soldiers knocking down doors in the middle of the night and dragging the laird and lady from their bedrooms in the tower, and apparently many of the wild tales were true. Torcall Castle had seen its share of dastardly deeds.

Nicholas said, "She mentioned Malcolm for a reason, and therefore he figures into the game somehow. Let's enlist the girls for our Christmas treasure hunt and develop a plan. The clock's ticking, as Mother said. Tiona, what did you want to say earlier?"

"Has any of you been to your bedroom?"

None had, and she described the bizarre transformation she found. "Same for your room, Nicky," she added. "I stuck my head inside — your old rugby team cup, the Beatles poster Father let you hang on the wall because John Lennon autographed it — everything's back like it was. It's your old room again."

"That's impossible. She redecorated all the rooms after we left. You saw them when you came for the funeral."

"That's my point. Argue all you want, but I think you should go take a look. Then you can tell me how impossible it is."

THE LAST CHRISTMAS

Nicholas, Carly and Noelle left Tiona alone in the great room for perhaps ten minutes. When they returned, Nicholas said, "You're absolutely right. Who...how would someone have gone to the trouble to recreate our childhood bedrooms? Tiona, your mother owes us an explanation."

Noelle raised her eyebrows. "Ask away, but I'll bet you a twenty you don't get answers."

CHAPTER ELEVEN

Benevolence Dayne's three grandchildren couldn't have been more different, thanks to their upbringing. Her stepson Nicholas was a New York investment banker who started his own firm, weathered one financial storm after another, and emerged a multimillionaire. Thanks to an active publicity team, people recognized him easily.

His daughters, Stephanie and Jillian, grew up in luxury on the Upper East Side. Today Steph was nineteen and a sophomore at New York University, and Jill was a sixteen-year-old junior attending an exclusive private school in midtown.

Noelle Dayne's early adult years differed vastly from her brother's. At eighteen she married Mitchell Curzon, a dashing but unambitious man and a distant relative of an aristocratic, wealthy family. They settled in London, where Mitchell also went into banking. Unlike his entrepreneurial brother-in-law, Mitchell was a salaried clerk who toiled in a sub-basement at the Bank of England on Threadneedle Street.

Noelle worked her way up from barista to manager of the Pret A Manger in Piccadilly, but still they struggled to pay the rent on their tiny flat in east London. When she turned up pregnant, it was bad timing, and their daughter, Poppy, was left to her own devices most of the time.

Poppy was sixteen when her father moved out and her mother suffered a nervous breakdown. She dropped out of school and moved away. When her parents divorced in 2019, she was twenty-two and hadn't spoken to either of them in six years.

Since their arrival at Torcall Castle, Poppy had been thrown with the rich bitches, a moniker she gave them after looking at the clothes they wore and the top-of-the-line tablets and phones they carried. Content to use an older phone and tablet, she kept her thoughts to herself.

Poppy had to endure chatter about boyfriends, school classes, an upcoming spring break trip to Hong Kong, and the Ferrari convertible their dad kept at their summer house in the Hamptons. When Poppy didn't respond, it signaled to Steph and Jill she had nothing to add, and they continued as if she weren't there.

In another time and place, Poppy might have revealed what her own life was like, something not even her mother was aware of. If she told them, it would blow these airheads away, and she wished she could do it. Right now — during Christmas at her grandmother's castle in Scotland — didn't seem the time to disclose what a black sheep this family had.

She worked five nights a week at the Flexin' Vixen, a nude bar and lap-dance joint just blocks away from her mother's wine bar in Soho. A pole dancer with a killer figure, she wasn't reluctant to take wealthy clients to the back room, and some nights she ended her eight-hour shift with over a thousand pounds in her pocket.

"Kids, come down. We need to talk to you." His daughters bitched when they heard their father's command.

"Come on, guys," Poppy said. "We're supposed to be on holiday. I don't care for my mother a whit, but 'tis the season and all that." She led the others down the stairs and into the great room, where Nicholas described the cryptic riddle and the treasure — or whatever it was — that must be found by sundown on Boxing Day.

"I pass," Jill said, rising from the couch with a yawn. "I'll be upstairs if anyone needs me."

Stephanie stood too, and their father said, "Sit down, both of you. You're going to help us, because this is important. Maybe it'll be fun too, even more than burying your face in an iPad. We need every person working together. We're uncertain what we're looking for, but it's worth a million pounds or more."

Poppy asked how they could find something without knowing what it was.

"Your grandmother gave us the clues. I presume they'll allow us to solve the puzzle. We just have to interpret them."

Noelle suggested reading the clues again one by one, allowing everyone to comment on each. Tiona disagreed, saying they should consider the list in total, because some seemed to go together.

"What do you mean?" Poppy asked, and Nicholas handed her the list.

"Read them aloud for us, please."

She read them first to herself, saying, "Tiona, I agree with you. There are similar ones. Here we go. *I watched each of you grow, although I held my tongue about what I saw. Although I often communicated, I never spoke.* Those two clues go together. So do the ones about him being older than anyone living today, and having seen wars, rebellions, royalty and treasure."

Carly said, "The clues are about a thing, because a person would be hundreds of years old."

Nicholas disagreed. "Consider the ghost stories about this castle. Uncle Malcolm Dayne fits, and Benevolence even suggested enlisting his help, which on the surface makes no sense. But what if it does make sense somehow? He'd be almost three hundred years old now — older than anyone living today. He was involved in the Jacobite Rebellion, and he hid Bonnie Prince Charlie here before he fled Scotland. Charles was the Stuart claimant to the throne who would have been King Charles III, so he could be the royal the clue mentioned."

That dialogue got everyone's attention, and Poppy said, "I have an idea about the name Mary being significant. I remember as a little girl coming here and sitting on Grandfather's knee while he told stories about Torcall Castle. One I still remember was about a real queen coming to visit. He said Mary, Queen of Scots, stayed in the castle for two nights in the fifteen hundreds. Perhaps she's the royal and the reason the name Mary is important."

"Now that's a possibility," Nicholas said. "I heard that story too — we all did. It's an interesting tale passed down through the generations. There's a book in the library — a history of the Dayne clan from the fourteen hundreds to around 1850. The book fascinated me as a teenager, and I remember reading all about Mary's visit."

Poppy said, "We can't be certain if that's the Mary in the clue, but she's likely the most significant Mary who ever visited. How can we find out which room she slept in, or if something important happened while she was here?"

"Let me go look for that book," Nicholas said. "But let's finish the clues first. There's only one left — the second one. Tiona, please read it again."

Numbers are very important to me. They are my life.

"Ideas?" Noelle said, and Jill asked if he might have been a mathematician.

"He could have been a scientist or physicist, an astronomer or astrologer," Tiona offered. "Or perhaps a magician. They considered certain numbers lucky and others cursed."

Noelle suggested thinking outside the box. What if the subject of the clues was an inanimate object, *something* instead of *someone*?

"That would make no sense," Poppy said. "The clue says numbers are very important and are my life. A *thing* can't consider something important; therefore it's a person."

Steph disagreed with her cousin. The clue didn't say the subject *considered* numbers important. It merely said that numbers *were* important — the most important thing of all to him…or it.

"You're splitting hairs, sis," Jill said. "Nothing can be important to a thing. Would a teapot care how old it was? Or at what temperature water boiled? No. It just sits there and does whatever it's supposed to do."

Nicholas returned with a thick, leather-bound volume, laid it on a table, and opened it. The worn, dog-eared pages revealed how many Dayne family members had turned to this book for a glimpse into the clan's history.

He thumbed through pages until he came to the chapter he wanted. He smiled as he read an inscription written in pencil at the top of its first page.

Nicholas Stuart Dayne read this story. August 17, 1987.

Steph said, "Nice handwriting, Dad. How old were you then?"

"Let's see. Thirteen. I was thirteen years old, and the word was penmanship, not handwriting. Father hired a tutor to teach us how to write like aristocrats."

"And that was exactly the word he used," Noelle added. "I never knew I was an aristocrat until Father drummed it into my head."

He flipped another few pages and read aloud about the laird's delight when he learned that the queen planned a visit. There was a lot to do in a few months' time, and the master of Torcall Castle spared no expense.

"Girls, are you aware which tower was named for Mary?"

Noelle smiled. Of course she and Tiona knew — they'd grown up within these walls like Nicholas, and they'd spent hours as children climbing the stairs to see what remained of the ruined Queen's Tower.

The grandchildren — Steph, Jill and Poppy — had no idea, and Nicholas took them to the window. "See that round building over there a hundred yards across the courtyard? In the fifteen hundreds it stood sixty feet tall, and when our ancestor learned the monarch intended to visit, he refurbished the ancient tower and added an enormous clock. The book says the chiming of each hour echoed through the hills and valleys and into the village two miles away."

"It's nothing but a heap of rubble today," Jill said, and her father explained that the English had destroyed it and other parts of the castle in the mid-1700s. He flipped to that part of the family history and read another account.

"They destroyed the Queen's Tower, and they'd have hauled off the clock if they could, but at twelve feet in diameter, they had no way to carry it. According to the person who wrote this in 1770, it still lies up there somewhere in the ruins."

Tiona had been sitting by the fire, half-listening to Nicholas give the children a history lesson. Without warning, she stood and said, "The clock. That's it!"

Noelle asked what she was talking about.

"Let's read the clues again and see if they might fit the clock."

Nicholas paraphrased each one. It watched them grow without saying a word. Numbers are its life. It's older than anyone living today and has seen wars and rebellions, royalty and treasure. It often communicated — that's the chime every hour, he opined — but it never "spoke." Mary is a name of great significance, and of course it would be to the clock that was installed in the Queen's Tower in honor of Mary's visit.

"Tiona, you may be right. The clues seem to fit, so we should look there first. The last clue says, 'I hold a secret of immense value.' Who knows what that means? Perhaps we can find the clock, even in a tower that's been in ruins since the middle of the eighteenth century."

Carly said, "Remember what your mother said? You'd better get to work because the clock is ticking. Do you think that was about the clock?"

"Perhaps it was a cleverly disguised clue of its own. That old clock hasn't ticked in centuries, but it might hold a clue. Let's get our rain gear and meet in the kitchen in fifteen minutes."

As they ran across the courtyard in the driving rain, two people watched from a tower window. "They're going to the Queen's Tower, thinking they've already figured things out. They haven't yet, of course, but they're moving more quickly than I expected," Benevolence said.

The man nodded. "But what they've done so far is the simple part. They have less than three days to finish, and I'll wager even with seven of them trying, they won't find what they're after. I still question the wisdom of bringing them here."

Benevolence said, "It's over and done. Here they are, and I agree they won't reach their goal without help. Your help." As he objected, she raised her hand and stopped him. "All right, all right. You're precluded from helping. But surely there are things you can do. It means everything to both of us, Malcolm."

CHAPTER TWELVE

The wind whipped the rain into sheets that blew sideways as Nicholas and the others ran across the grassy rectangular courtyard. Before them stood the ruins of the Queen's Tower, one of four that had protected the castle for over five hundred years. The English had stormed Torcall Castle in 1746 after defeating the Jacobites at Culloden, and they'd destroyed much, including the top two-thirds of the Queen's Tower.

Fifty feet in diameter and fifteen feet tall, the bottom story remained intact, a symbol of strength and resistance. Above lay the ruined part — the jumbled mess of enormous stones. The tower was unsafe, and for over two hundred years Dayne children were forbidden from venturing inside. That warning was a temptation, and Nicholas was certain every child raised here crawled through the rubble and explored the old tower just as he and his siblings had done.

Earlier, Noelle had asked if anyone recalled seeing the clock when they had gone exploring in the ruins as youngsters. None did, although Tiona said perhaps it lay high in the tower. They might never have seen it or forgotten it was there.

Boards covered the entrance where a solid oak door once stood, and they pulled away enough to squeeze through single file. Tiona ducked inside last, turning to look back to the tower they'd just left. She noticed movement in a top window. The weather made for poor visibility, but she thought she made out two figures. She stepped inside, glanced again, and saw nothing.

They gathered in the round room whose stone walls formed the tower's base. A wide stone staircase wound up one wall, and they took it to the next level. Rubble from above had crashed through the ceiling — also the floor of the third level — and through holes they saw grey clouds. Massive stones lay in heaps, leaving no way to explore what might lie beneath.

With rubble strewn everywhere, the next flight of stairs was tricky to navigate. After a few slips, curses and saves, they emerged into open air almost twenty feet above the ground. Grass grew between great piles of stones, and with much difficulty the most agile among them — the three young girls — scaled the rocks, searched in vain for a clock, and returned to the others.

"But the kids only saw the surface," Noelle reminded the others. "It could be buried beneath tons of stones, out of sight and impossible to retrieve."

Everyone agreed further searching was fruitless without equipment. They returned to their rooms for showers and a change of clothes, and at the appointed cocktail hour they assembled in the great room.

A moment later, Benevolence walked in and took her usual chair near the fireplace, some distance from the others.

"Good evening, Mother," Tiona said. "Why don't you sit over here where it's easier to talk?"

"I can talk here just fine." She rang the little bell to alert Mrs. Campbell about cocktail time. "What have you been up to since I left you?"

Tiona said, "Tell us about the bedrooms, Mother. How did you pull that off?"

She paused as if to collect her thoughts and then said, "I don't know what you're talking about."

Nicholas snapped, "Benevolence, we're not children. You can't pretend nothing happened upstairs, and I want an explanation."

Benevolence looked past them at a tall, rugged man who stood in shadows at the back of the room — the person Tiona had seen in the upstairs window earlier — and as the family pushed her for answers, the man gave Benevolence a nod and a smile.

His expression seemed to give Benevolence resolve. "The castle is haunted. You heard stories as children, I heard them when I married your father, and they are all true. These old walls have seen many joys and sorrows over the past six hundred years, and were your father here, he might explain the unusual things that happen at Torcall Castle. I cannot. I was as perplexed as you when the rooms changed in an instant. I oversaw the renovations myself. It made no sense.

"All I can say is, someone or something didn't care for the remodeling. One day without warning Mrs. Campbell discovered what had happened, and it terrified both of us, but the ghost of Torcall Castle assured me everything was fine."

The man in the back of the room beamed with delight and gave her a thumbs-up.

"The ghost?" Steph said. "Does it still come around?"

"Oh yes, but the ghost will do you no harm. Quite the contrary, he protects the Dayne family."

"Who is he? Or was he, I mean?"

"The most famous clan chief of all. Malcolm Dayne. The warrior who hid Bonnie Prince Charlie here after the defeat at Culloden in 1746. If you're lucky enough to meet him while you're here, thank him for guarding the castle and the family all these years."

While they struggled to process her revelations and asked more questions, Benevolence had had enough. "I've told you all I know about your bedrooms, and I've revealed we have a resident spirit. Now we'll talk about something else. What progress did you make this afternoon?"

Jill said, "We went to the Queen's Tower, Grandmother. We looked for an old clock."

She smiled. "So you joined forces. As competitive as you all are, I didn't think you'd do it. You know a clock once hung in the tower. Why do you consider it important?"

"Several of the clues pointed us in that direction," Poppy said. "Were we right?"

She ignored the question. "Did you find the clock?"

"No. If it's there, it's buried beneath the stones."

Moments later, as Laris pushed the drink trolley into the room, the man who had stood in the back disappeared.

Nicholas admitted he was stumped, at least for the moment. It seemed the clues were about the clock, but they hadn't found it. He asked for ideas about what to do next. The old woman listened as they tossed out ideas and suggestions, but nothing seemed good enough, and an hour later when it was dinnertime, they were still at a loss on how to proceed.

CHAPTER THIRTEEN

The seating arrangement was identical to that at lunch, with Benevolence seated beside Nicholas. Laris and Mrs. Campbell served a seven-course meal with twice as much food as they could have eaten. They managed by consuming small portions of plate after plate the servants put in front of them.

When they had finished and the dishes cleared, Mrs. Campbell offered tea. Several accepted, but Nicholas said he'd take a brandy in the library instead. "Is Father's old humidor still stocked with cigars?" he asked his mother.

Freshly stocked, she said. Last week Barclay had brought up a box of her husband's favorite cigars from the castle's crypt. In its cool, moist environment, Geoffrey Dayne had built a humidor and wine cellar.

As Mrs. Campbell poured tea, Tiona asked her if she'd ever heard of a secret hidden in the tower clock. The woman's sudden reaction took them all by surprise. Her hand trembled, she spilled a little tea, and Steph shouted as scalding liquid dripped on her arm.

"I'm so sorry, Miss Stephanie," the poor housekeeper said, dabbing the spot with a towel. "May I get you a bandage?"

Steph assured her it was nothing to worry about, but in the hubbub, Tiona's question went unanswered. Moments later, Nicholas excused himself, and Noelle followed her brother into the library. Here, as in the great room, a cozy fire burned in the hearth, its shadows flickering upon dark wood bookshelves that rose to the ceiling. She chose a chair near the fire, and he walked to a desk on which an antique humidor decorated with inlaid silver sat. It had belonged to his great-grandfather, and it reminded him of his sixteenth birthday, when his father had offered him his first cigar.

"Will you join me?" he joked, and it surprised him when she accepted. He chose two Cohiba Talismans, handed one and a sterling silver cutter to Noelle, and soon they were taking the first puffs of the exquisite Cuban cigars.

"I suppose you'll have a brandy as well?" he said, and she nodded. He walked across the room, opened a corner cabinet, and surveyed the contents. He selected a bottle and showed it to Noelle.

"I'll be damned," he exclaimed. "This is Louis XIII cognac. Almost full. It wasn't here when we came for the funeral nine years ago, but someone with excellent taste ensured we'd have a rare treat."

"I'm not familiar with it," she said, and he called it one of the world's great brandies. As he poured, he added, "At my club in New York, a snifter like this will set you back three hundred dollars."

"At my pub, we don't have snifters. Brandy either."

He asked his sister how her life was going, and she confessed she often struggled to survive. The Goose and Gander occupied prime space in busy Leicester Square, with a street-level entrance and a cozy bar and dining room at the bottom of a circular staircase. Thousands of tourists passed by every day, and major train stations nearby allowed locals to pop in for a drink before going home. Despite all that, Noelle had trouble making ends meet.

Nicholas quizzed her about cash flow, her prices versus her costs for food and drink, and how her liquor distribution system worked. He'd seen unaccountable bartenders serve free liquor to customers who tipped well, a practice that could ruin a business with thin margins. His sister had a good grasp of the business side of her enterprise, and he asked how much time she spent at the pub. The owner's watchful eye was often all that kept the staff on the straight and narrow.

"I live there, for God's sake," she replied. "I open the place, I close it, and the only break I get is Saturdays, when I don't come in until four. It's dragging me down, to tell the truth. I work far too hard for the meager profit I generate. There has to be an easier way to make a living."

Her brother said, "I'd be happy to help you, look at the books, staffing, purchasing, cost versus pricing — that sort of thing. I'm no publican, but I understand how profitable businesses should run."

There was a knock on the door, and Mrs. Campbell popped in to ask if they required anything more. Laris and John had left for their quarters in the gatehouse, and she, Cook and Barclay were retiring soon to their rooms in the castle.

"We're fine," Nicholas said, thanking her for all she had done for them today. Then he had a thought. "If you have a moment, I'd like to ask something. In your opinion, how is our stepmother getting along? She's always been eccentric, as we all know, but this time is different. She keeps her distance and seems more aloof than ever."

The woman's eyes darted here and there, and they expressed her feelings better than the hollow words. "Lady Dayne seems just fine to me," she said. "Of course, I'm with her every day, and you haven't seen her in nine years. Perhaps there is something, but I'm afraid I'm not the one to ask. Now if there's nothing else I'll take my leave…"

Noelle said, "There is something else. Her story about the bedrooms suddenly transforming themselves can't be true, so how did she do it? They were redecorated when we came for Father's funeral. Now everything's back as it was fifty years ago. What's that about, Mrs. Campbell?"

She picked at a fingernail. "I don't know. You shouldn't ask me such questions. It's none of my business. These are family things — things to ask her about yourself without involving me."

Noting the old housekeeper's distress, Noelle apologized and changed the subject. "What's hidden in the Queen's Tower?"

Mrs. Campbell stammered, "Hidden? Uh, I'm not supposed to — that is, it's not my place to discuss things with you. You are family; I'm staff. And about the tower — I know nothing about the clock." She turned to go, but Nicholas stopped her.

"No one mentioned a clock. Sit with us, Mrs. Campbell. There seems to be a lot you might tell us — even things you aren't supposed to talk about. I'm lord of the estate and therefore your employer, so indulge me and my sister. Help us understand what's going on here."

CHAPTER FOURTEEN

Reluctantly the housekeeper sat, stared off into space, and said, "Please, Nicholas. I can't help you."

"Can't or won't?" he asked the woman he'd known from birth. "We don't want to put you in an awkward position. I'm not asking you to reveal confidences about her, but I want answers. Things are different in the castle. You, Cook and Barclay, for instance. You must be almost ninety, but you haven't aged a day since I saw you nine years ago. Our bedrooms have become the rooms of our youth, and we're off on a bizarre scavenger hunt that I'm convinced involves the tower clock. Talk to us, Mrs. Campbell."

She surprised them by standing, walking across the room, and pouring herself two fingers of the cognac. She returned, sat, took a deep sip, and said, "I hope you won't think badly of me. I know how dear the laird's brandy is, and I swear I've never nicked a drop before. It's just that…" She paused and took another sip, the liquid moving about in the snifter as her hand trembled.

"Think nothing of it," Nicholas said with a smile. "Who am I to cast aspersions on an after-dinner drink to soothe one's nerves?"

"Lady Dayne would not approve of my speaking to you."

Noelle assured her the conversation would go no further than this room. They had no intention of causing problems for the housekeeper. They had been here half a day, and already they'd encountered puzzling things that required explanation.

"The castle is haunted."

Noelle glanced at her brother. "Benevolence told us the same thing earlier. And when we were children, Father told us stories of the spirits that haunted Torcall Castle. I saw ghostly shadows in these halls myself, Nicky. Did you?"

I saw more than that, he thought, but kept it to himself. "Children have vivid imaginations. I gave up the fantasies of youth when I reached adulthood. I don't believe in ghosts now."

Noelle shot him a look and sneered, "Pardon me, milord. I forgot whose presence I was in. Aren't we getting a little big for our kilt?"

"Sorry, I didn't mean it like that. Of course I imagined seeing things back then. Growing up in a six-hundred-year-old castle, who wouldn't? But back to you, Mrs. Campbell. Have you seen ghosts?"

"I have, many times. There are several, but one appears most often. One time he'll be in the library, another time standing high in the ruins of the tower. He does your family proud in his Dayne tartan kilt with his dirk sheathed in a scabbard on his belt."

"Malcolm Dayne?" Noelle asked. "Benevolence said he was the resident ghost."

"That he is. Malcolm risked his life for the Jacobite cause and Charles Stuart, the rightful king, and he stood up to the Redcoats when they came looking for Charles. They destroyed half of the castle, but thanks to Malcolm, the rest stands today. He was a warrior and a genuine hero."

"How can you be certain it's him?"

The old housekeeper smiled. "If you meet him, you'll know."

Nicholas said, "I asked you about strange events here, and you instead spoke of ghosts in the castle. Tell us more."

"About what, Lord Dayne? What are you asking of me?"

"Your age, for starters. Pardon my asking a lady's age, but how old are you?"

"Seventy-eight."

Nicholas did a quick mental calculation. "Please, Mrs. Campbell. That's impossible. I'm sixty-seven. You were at least twenty when I was a toddler, so you are at least in your late eighties. You look seventy-eight, I'll grant you that, but you're not. Explain, please."

She paused, took another drink of the cognac and stammered, "It's not that simple. You wouldn't understand…"

"I'm fairly bright. Try me."

She started to speak, paused and stammered, "I cannot violate a sacred trust. You were summoned home for Christmas, and you must be gone by Boxing Day at sundown. Nothing here is as it seems. Perhaps you will be told certain things; that is not for me to say. You must accept things as you see them, and not as you might expect them to be. I'm sorry, Nicholas, but I won't say anything more. Please, may I go now?" She stood and waited.

"Please stay a moment longer. Your reticence makes it clear you're keeping someone's secrets, probably my stepmother's. Tell us about the Queen's Tower and this treasure hunt of hers. Is our ancestor Malcolm Dayne involved in it?"

The woman's eyes darted here and there as tongues of flame from the fireplace created eerie, undulating figures on the walls. She looked about carefully as if searching for something, then looked into his eyes.

"I must be careful," she whispered. "They don't appreciate gossip about their secrets, milord."

"Who are *they*? The ghosts?"

"The tower was part of the original castle built in the fourteen hundreds. When the laird learned Mary, Queen of

Scots, was coming for a visit, he installed an enormous clock and renamed it the Queen's Tower. The clock rang the hour across the hills and valleys for almost two hundred years until the Redcoats destroyed the tower.

"Earlier today, I saw you fetch the Dayne family history book from the library. I've looked at that old volume many times over the years. You can read about what happened to the clock after the English stormed Torcall Castle. All I can tell you is this — the Queen's Tower is not where you should search. The clock…"

A sharp rap came on the door, and Barclay entered, wearing a satin robe over his pajamas. In other circumstances, they would have smiled at his rare lack of formality. Tonight he was all business, and he frowned when he saw them together.

"Mrs. Campbell, what are you doing in here?" he snapped. "Lady Dayne's been ringing the bell for fifteen minutes. At last she roused me out of bed to come find you. She wishes to see you in her quarters."

"Dear God," she cried. "Barclay, please don't tell her I was here. She'll be furious with me."

"I won't bring it up," he said, "but I won't lie for you either. Then again, I'm not the one to be concerned about, Mrs. Campbell. If *he* told her you're in the library, then she already knows."

The woman fled the room, straightening her apron and running toward the staircase. Barclay looked at the table where her drink sat, picked up the glass, and shook his head. "Staff may not socialize with the family."

Nicholas said, "Barclay, for God's sake, it's the twenty-first century. The staff can socialize with whoever they want. I asked her to join us. I've known both of you since I was a boy, and we were reminiscing about old times."

"Regardless, Lady Dayne will not be happy should she learn of Mrs. Campbell's…" He stopped before he said the word *indiscretion.*

"You said someone else might tell Benevolence. A man. Who were you talking about?"

He trembled as he backed toward the door. "Begging your pardon. I'm as out of line as Mrs. Campbell. I'm an old fool who speaks when he shouldn't. I meant nothing by it. Sleep well."

Noelle cried, "Barclay, don't leave. You didn't answer Nicky!"

The door closed and the man was gone.

"What impertinence!" Noelle said.

"He's not impertinent. He's afraid of something."

CHAPTER FIFTEEN

Mrs. Campbell stood outside the door that led into Benevolence Dayne's quarters. She would rather have taken a beating than to walk in there, not because of the berating she deserved from her employer, but because of everything else.

Nothing was the same now that the staff had to tiptoe around the truth and pretend things hadn't changed. In another time she'd have tendered her resignation, but after what had happened a year ago, such a thought was ludicrous.

Before that day, Mrs. Campbell considered herself in an enviable position. She had work and a roof over her head; her salary and money for household expenses came by courier from the Glasgow accounting firm every week without fail; and she lacked for nothing. Until that fateful evening, she ran the castle without interference from Lady Dayne. Today her work continued, but now she was bound forever to the castle and the Dayne family. She couldn't leave.

She knocked, listened to a muffled response, and opened the heavy door into Lady Dayne's boudoir. She entered, hoping her mistress would be in this room. But instead, she received a summons to come into the next one.

The housekeeper took a deep breath before stepping into the dark bedroom. She hadn't had to come here for months. As her personal maid, Laris tended the bedroom and handled Lady Dayne's personal needs, which suited Mrs.

Campbell just fine. The room had always given her goosebumps.

She knew what to expect and held her breath, but exhaled when she announced herself. As she drew in her next breath, the odd, sickly-sweet smell triggered her gag reflex. She coughed and covered her mouth and nose with her hand. She knew that odor — she lived with it herself — but on another person, it was nauseating.

"Milady, how may I assist?"

"You may *assist* by telling me why you went into the library with my stepchildren. Under the circumstances, do you consider that a wise move, Mrs. Campbell?"

"I…it was nothing, madam. I popped in to be sure they didn't need anything else for the evening and…"

Without thinking, she moved toward the bed as she spoke, and Benevolence said, "Stop. Come no closer!"

"Yes, milady." The woman lowered her eyes, uncomfortable to be alone with the mistress in her private quarters.

"What did they ask? Don't lie, because he was there. He heard and saw everything."

Mrs. Campbell hadn't seen him while they sat in the library, but she knew Lady Dayne was telling the truth. The man moved about the castle undetected, and no staff member was safe from his eyes and ears. That old warrior from long ago, in his tartan plaid kilt. Malcolm Dayne, protecting his clan even to this day.

"Begging your pardon, madam. Nicholas…er, Lord Dayne that is, ordered me to sit for a moment. He wanted to know about the clock in the tower. He said they are trying to solve a puzzle you presented to them."

"You told them Malcolm Dayne haunts this castle, and you told them not to look in the Queen's Tower."

"If he told you that, it's a lie. I didn't tell him —"

"You didn't finish because Barclay interrupted you. I sent them on a mission, something important to the future of the Dayne clan and this castle. I would appreciate if you would henceforth refrain from interjecting yourself into affairs not your own. Now go."

The housekeeper stood in the hallway a moment, gasping breaths of clean, fresh air before walking toward the wing that held the servants' quarters. The tall man in the kilt watched her from the half-light outside Benevolence's door. When Mrs. Campbell rounded the corner, he passed through it noiselessly.

In the library, Noelle and Nicholas tried to understand what had happened. The housekeeper had been about to reveal something about the clock, Barclay summoned her to their stepmother's room, and the woman looked like the cops caught her robbing a bank.

And there was the puzzling comment about a man. How did Barclay put it? *If* he *told her you're in the library.*

"We and Mrs. Campbell were the only people here," Noelle said. "Why did Barclay mention a man overhearing the conversation? The only other man in the castle is Laris's husband, John, and he had left for the gatehouse earlier."

"The ghost, I suppose. Let's get that old Dayne history book and see what more we can learn about the clock."

CHAPTER SIXTEEN

Carly was snoring as Nicholas slipped under the duvet. It was nearing midnight and he tried to sleep, but the strange events in the library plagued his thoughts. He believed in ghosts — what good Scot didn't? — and this spooky castle provided a perfect site for a supernatural encounter. Its cold stone halls seemed to go on forever past tall doors that opened to rooms filled with six centuries of Dayne memorabilia.

As would any child growing up in a medieval castle, young Nicholas had done his share of exploring, but there remained rooms he'd never seen and areas among the ruins he hadn't gone. Had he seen a ghost in those days? He thought perhaps so, but then again it could have been a vision precipitated by the spooky tales his father spun and the ancient castle where he lived.

As the housekeeper had predicted, the family's history book provided clues about Malcolm Dayne's connection to the ruined Queen's Tower and where the clock might be today. When he flipped to another page, Nicholas found something even more interesting — a spellbinding tale about a centuries-old lost treasure.

Nicholas didn't recall reading that account before, but the flourishes and swirls of the aristocratic hand that penned the legend fascinated Noelle and him. With only two days remaining on their invitation, this story would have to wait. There simply wasn't time. He and his sister agreed to join forces, come back to Torcall someday, and hunt for treasure.

Only two years apart in age — today he was sixty-seven and she sixty-five — as children they had been inseparable. They were Nicky and Noe back then. After their mother passed, Father had married a Pennsylvania Quaker named Benevolence Townsend. Sixteen years younger, she gave him two more children, Tiona, now forty-six, and Aidan, thirty-nine. Nicolas and Noelle were already at university when they arrived, and they had no familial and little social connection with their half-siblings.

I enjoyed talking to my sister tonight. We haven't done that in so long. I'm in London on business twice a month. I should have looked her up before now, met for lunch, had a pint — something. But I was busy, the time flew by, and each time I flew back to New York without seeing her. It won't be that way going forward. Time's passing and we should stay in contact.

At last he slept, but something woke him. A series of knocking sounds, faint and muffled — probably something banging in the wind. He got out of bed, walked to the window and looked out into the courtyard. The rain appeared to have stopped, but low clouds made the enclosure so dark it was impossible to see even the ruined tower across the way.

As he returned to bed, he noticed movement across the room. Something wispy swirled around the door, and in seconds a figure formed from the misty vapors. A tall man wearing a Glengarry tam and a tartan kilt looked at him with dark, fierce eyes. A scabbard with a knife hung from his belt, and Nicholas realized this was the ghost Mrs. Campbell had reported seeing many times in the house. He also remembered this fearsome figure from his childhood. His fierce demeanor created no dread; instead, Nicholas felt kinship with this rugged Scotsman who was his ancestor.

The spirit glided across the room to where Nicholas stood. A mighty man with unruly hair and beard and fire in his eyes, he was a dashing, swashbuckling figure who looked as if he could overpower his foes without batting an eye. The hair rose on Nicholas's arms as his relative from past centuries spoke.

Careful not to wake Carly, he whispered, "Greetings, Malcolm."

"Greetings to you. You're the laird."

"Yes, whatever that means these days. Why are you here, Uncle? You've been..." He paused, unsure how to broach the subject of death with a ghost.

"I've been in the crypt for over two hundred years, but it's not my fate to lie peacefully in my coffin."

"Why is that?"

His clothing and body shimmered in the darkness, creating an eerie but not unpleasant sensation. "I made a pact with the devil. When the Redcoats came and destroyed half the castle, I promised him my soul if he'd save the Dayne family and their ancestral home. 'Done,' auld Clootie says with a snap of his fingers. 'So long as a clan chief lives at Torcall, the castle will be spared.' And to this day, it has been so. Old Satan mockingly dubbed me 'Chief Protector,' and even in death that is my duty. It's my lot to protect Torcall Castle for as long as it stands."

"From whom?"

"From the English, damn their hides."

"But that's over and done with."

"In your world, milord, but not in mine. I killed Redcoats in the courtyard just outside your window. They attacked the castle, and I shot them dead. I buried them where they lay, unwittingly giving them license to haunt the castle. They wanted bloody Christian burials, and I gave them a hole in the ground. They cannot rest, nor can I. I doomed myself to be the protector of the Dayne family for eternity. Damn me!" He laughed so loudly Nicholas turned to see if Carly had awakened. Her light breathing proved only he could hear the spirit.

"So your job for eternity is to protect the castle and our family from its enemies?"

The phantom nodded. "Aye. The Redcoats aren't the only ones to worry about. Torcall Castle is ancient. It was three hundred years old when I was alive, and it's nigh on six hundred now. Over the centuries evil men and women — including some of your own ancestors, milord — committed atrocities against enemies perceived and actual. People died inside the castle. The ruined parts contain resting places for some who were entombed in walls and floors. Even the extant part where we stand has hauntings of its own."

Nicholas remembered other parts of his childhood — seeing fleeting glimpses of wispy figures far down a hallway, or turning a corner just as someone vanished, or waking to see shadows in his bedroom. "So you protected Noelle and me as we grew up?"

"Aye. They hate the Daynes, and that's a fact, but I've kept them at bay."

"Are they dangerous? Will they harm us?"

"I'll be on the lookout," the spirit assured him. "I'll come if I'm needed, but I wouldn't worry about them physically assaulting anyone. It's unlikely you'll see anyone but me. If you do, they'll just try to scare you."

Nicholas thanked him for watching out for the family and asked what he knew about the clock that once hung in the Queen's Tower.

"What is it ye want to know?"

"A secret. Benevolence gave us a set of clues that seem to point to the clock and something valuable."

"I'm aware milady gave you a game to play. She told me about it, and she explained why it was important for all of you to gather one last time. Things are not as they seem. Not with her, or with her clues, or the clock, the servants, or even with me. You have much more to learn before you unveil the secrets. It's your destiny as the lord of Torcall Castle. Everything depends on it."

"Mrs. Campbell used your same words — things are not as they seem. What are you talking about? I don't understand."

"And you won't, milord. Not until it's time. Now you must go downstairs. There are guests at the front door."

He glanced at his watch. Two twenty. "Guests at this hour?" he said, but the apparition had disappeared.

CHAPTER SEVENTEEN

Nicholas donned a robe and descended the enormous stairway. The house was dark and quiet, and he wondered if the spirit had sent him on a wild-goose chase. He pulled aside two heavy bolts and turned the metal key that rested in the lock.

In the entryway, sheltered from the wind and rain, lay two sleeping bags. A head stuck out of each, and the occupants opened bleary eyes as they realized someone was there.

"Hello, Nicky."

"Aidan, is that you? What on earth are you doing out here?"

"The castle was dark, and since it's late, we decided not to disturb you. We walked from Mallaig. Oh, this is Izzy — Isabella, my girlfriend. Izzy, this is my brother, Nicholas."

"Oh, the one you call the lord of the manor." The sarcasm was bitter. "I've never met a royal before."

Aidan apologized to Nicholas and snapped, "He's not a royal. He's the clan chief."

"La-di-da. Never met one of those either."

Surprised and irritated, Nicholas said, "I hate to interrupt this fascinating conversation, but let's get you both inside where it's warm." He told them to toss the sleeping bags in a corner by the door and said they'd be staying in Aidan's childhood bedroom. "I trust you can find it," he added, and Aidan nodded. "Sleep as late as you want. I'll see you downstairs whenever you're up. Your mother has us on some kind of treasure hunt. I'll explain everything in the morning."

As Nicholas returned to his room and crawled into bed, Carly mumbled, "Where have you been? I thought I heard you talking to someone earlier."

"Aidan finally arrived with a girl in tow. A much younger girl who's a bit of a wiseass. They had camped out on the doorstep, and I went downstairs to let them in."

"How did you know they were there?"

"It's a long story," he said. "Go back to sleep. It'll keep 'til morning." He turned away and closed his eyes, but sleep eluded him for hours as he replayed the encounter with his ancestor.

CHAPTER EIGHTEEN

Christmas Eve — December 24

Dawn brought the sunshine. Yesterday's storms had blown out to sea, leaving western Scotland with the prospect of a frigid, dry and cloudless day. Aidan's breath came in frosty clouds as he walked an ancient path along the windswept coast that led to Torcall Village. He hadn't been there since he left Scotland in 1997, and he wondered how things had changed.

He broke into a grin as he entered the town and walked down its cobbled streets. Although the shops in the high street differed from those of his youth, the fifteenth- and sixteenth-century stone buildings that housed them remained the same. That was an aspect of Scotland he loved. In America, his adopted country, garish structures came down to make room for even more tasteless ones. Here in Scotland, people revered culture, history and tradition.

Aidan hadn't expected to find any shops open this early on a holiday morning. He'd invented a trip to town to have a break from Isabella rather than to buy something he'd forgotten. Aidan had known Izzy less than a month, and even this early, he realized bringing her to his ancestral home had been a mistake, but he was dead broke and his mother's invitation had mentioned money. Izzy had paid almost twelve thousand dollars for the tickets after Aidan promised to reimburse her from the money he got. Now that she was here and saw his family's ancestral home, he worried that she might create a problem.

Isabella was a twenty-four-year-old with a dynamite body. In small doses, she was fun to be with. They'd met in a seedy bar where she played guitar three nights a week. He bought her a drink and she invited him to her apartment for a quickie, which he laughed off, explaining that he didn't have the money. A few days later he learned turning tricks was Izzy's actual job, and she made far more money at it than he did dealing cards.

Kindred souls despite the age difference, they began hanging out on her nights off from the bar. He didn't know if she still brought men to her house, but he considered it none of his business. To each his own. That was her thing and he had no desire to run her life. All he wanted was a little unfettered companionship, and until this trip that was all their relationship had been.

The youngest of Geoffrey Dayne's children and the least successful in material terms, thirty-nine-year-old Aidan had jumped from one minimum-wage job to another, never staying long enough for a promotion or a pay raise. It wasn't that he was shiftless or incompetent; he simply didn't care. Every position became the means to an end, and he didn't need much. Whenever the job became a little stressful, or his boss offered more responsibility or a promotion, he bailed out. It meant living on minimum wage, but twenty thousand a year net bought a lot of nights in a tent under the stars, a thousand songs strummed on a used guitar, and days off spent hiking in New Mexico's glorious mountains.

Aidan turned a corner, walked into the village square, and smiled as he saw twinkling lights on an enormous Douglas fir standing in front of the old church. As always, his family would have provided the tree and paid someone to erect it, and on the first Sunday in December the entire town would have gathered to decorate it. He was glad that some things remained the same in a world that often discarded customs and traditions like crumpled wrapping paper.

In the middle of the square he saw the statue of Mary, Queen of Scots, erected in remembrance of her visit to the castle in the fifteen hundreds. The life-size icon sat on a base four feet tall, raising the monarch to a level befitting her station in life. How many times during his youth had he played with other youngsters around it? The fond memories caused him to smile.

A few other people were out this early — couples strolling hand in hand, a kid trying out his new bicycle, and a woman walking her dog — but he recognized no one. In the old days Aidan would have known many residents, and they would have known him, because most of the men worked on the Dayne estate. Back then the villagers were invited to the castle on Christmas Eve, where he and his family stood in a reception line and shook their hands. Each household left with a twenty-pound turkey. For some long-forgotten reason, that custom had been abandoned years ago and instead men delivered the turkeys to each home on December the twenty-third. Aidan smiled, thinking the townspeople must have been as relieved as the Dayne clan that the obligatory castle visits had ended.

Sarah's Sweet Shop. I'll be damned! There were lights shining through the front windowpanes! He rushed across the square and grinned when he opened the door and a little bell tinkled. He hadn't heard that sound in twenty-three years, yet it was as familiar as if it were yesterday.

Aidan always loved this place. As a child, he and his friends came here every day after school to buy penny candy or licorice or a Highland toffee bar. It looked and smelled much the same. The products were modern, of course, but in the back still stood the old soda fountain where you could sit on a stool that swiveled, and drink a soda that cost twenty pence.

"Hello? Is anyone here?"

"Be there in a sec," came a voice from the kitchen. "Have a look around."

Aidan did, and soon a girl appeared. Perhaps in her mid-thirties, she wore an apron on which she was drying her hands.

"Just making puddings," she said with a wide smile. "Sorry I didn't hear you come in. Merry Christmas to you."

Wow, she's beautiful. "And to you. I'm surprised you're open. I didn't expect —"

She interrupted gaily. "I had to work anyway, so I thought if I open up, perhaps someone will pick up a sweet as a last-minute gift. And here you are!"

"I came here often as a child," he said. "It was long before your time. Where is Sarah?"

"Sarah was my grandmother. She died ten years ago. I'm Ella." She stuck out her hand. "And who might you be?"

He paused a moment. "Aidan. My name's Aidan."

"And you say you lived in the village as a child? Where do you live now?"

"In America. I've lived there for many years."

"Wow!" she exclaimed. "You're a genuine tourist! We don't get many of those here in Torcall. What brings you to this remote place?"

Until now, Aidan had avoided revealing anything but his first name. If he said more, she'd realize she was talking to a member of the family who owned this village. Then again, why should he care?

"I came home for Christmas."

"How wonderful! It must thrill your family that you came from so far away. I'll wager I know your folks; no one's a stranger here in Torcall, as I'm sure you remember. What's your last name?"

"Dayne. I'm spending Christmas at the castle with my family."

Her eyes widened and she brought her hands to her face. "Oh my God. I'm so sorry. You're...you're Lord

Dayne? I didn't know, milord. I'm so sorry." She gave a little curtsy and lowered her eyes deferentially.

"Stop, please." He laughed. "My brother Nicholas is Lord Dayne. I'm Aidan, the youngest, and about as far from a Scottish lord as one can get."

"And the lord…is he at the castle as well?"

"Yes, he and his family came from New York. My sisters too. I apologize for startling you by revealing my name. I meant no harm. Did it shock you that Benevolence Dayne's children returned to the castle? It's been years, you know."

"No, sir. No, I'm not shocked that you're a Dayne. It was the other thing you said."

"That I was spending Christmas at the castle?"

"That, and that it was with your family. It must be terribly sad for all of you after the tragedy. I can't imagine what a depressing thing to face at Christmastime, especially there in the castle." She paused, saw the puzzled look on his face, and realized she had committed a major faux pas.

He doesn't know.

"Oh my, I'm so sorry. I never know when to shut up. I apologize, sir."

He smiled. "Please don't call me sir. I'm no different from you. Poorer, to be honest. At least you have a shop. Don't judge a book by its cover — or its title, in this case. Just because my name's Dayne doesn't mean I'm better than you or anyone else."

"Thank you, sir, I mean, Aidan. Thank you. Is there something I can get for you?" She struggled to change the subject, but it didn't work.

"You said how terribly sad it must be for all of us. I presume you're referring to the death of my father almost ten years ago. After a decade, any sadness is long gone. I haven't been back in ages. Neither have my siblings."

She knitted her brows and looked in his eyes. "I'm not speaking of your father. I'm talking about the tragedy.

93

The awful thing that happened at Torcall Castle last year at Christmas. They all — Dear God, you know, right? Please say you do. You *must* know. Benevolence Dayne. She...she was your mother, correct?"

"She *is* my mother, Ella. I arrived late last night, so I haven't seen her yet, but when I go back in a few minutes, she'll be holding court in the great room like always."

Ella shook her head, brushed away a tear, and stammered, "You really don't know? How can that be? You say you haven't been here in years, but surely someone notified you. It shouldn't fall upon me to be the bearer of such news."

The bell tinkled as the door opened and closed. To Ella's immense relief, a lady entered the shop.

"Mrs. Anderson," she called out, "I'll be right with you."

"Finish up with your customer, Ella. I'll just browse for a moment."

"I must go now," she told Aidan. "I'm sorry."

"Sorry for what? What on earth are you talking about?" His tone was stronger than he'd intended, and Mrs. Anderson glanced their way, wondering about the stranger who raised his voice at Ella.

The girl crossed herself and whispered, "They're dead, sir. Your mother, Benevolence, the cook, the housekeeper, and Barclay, the valet. The whole village knows about it. They all died on Boxing Day. Day after tomorrow it'll have been a year since their deaths. You won't be seeing your mother, because she's gone. I'm so, so sorry."

She walked away and left him speechless.

CHAPTER NINETEEN

His mind reeling, Aidan ran all the way back to Torcall Castle.

I've been out of touch. I've moved a dozen times. Perhaps the others couldn't reach me.

Nicky doesn't know either! Last night he said Benevolence has them on a treasure hunt. He spoke of her in the present tense. But how...and why?

And then something hit him.

If Mother is dead, who invited me home for Christmas? Who sent the letter?

None of it made sense.

Panting heavily, he threw open the front door and found Nicholas and his father's former valet, Barclay, chatting in the entry hall.

"Welcome home, Aidan," the butler said in a voice that sounded quite alive.

"Morning," Nicholas said. "What have you been up to? Isabella came down for breakfast half an hour ago. She said you walked to the village."

"I did. I wanted to see it after all these years." He was unable to stop staring at Barclay. What the hell was that girl Ella talking about? Was it some kind of sick joke?

"Where...where is Mother?" he asked, and Nicholas said she was in the great room with the others. "Come join us. Carly's here, and you've never met my daughters. It's been a long time."

Aidan took his brother's arm. "Not right now. Something happened in the village. I must speak to you in private. Barclay, please excuse us."

They passed the great room, where everyone sat sorting Christmas decorations and preparing to trim the tree. His mother, also looking fit and healthy, glanced up as he went by. The brothers went into the library, Aidan closed the door, and they sat. Nicholas observed the concern and distress on Aidan's face. Something was very wrong.

The moment the door closed, Barclay crept down the hall, looked each way to ensure he hadn't been seen, and cracked the door to listen. Aidan's going to the village had been a mistake that could result in dangerous consequences, and he must learn what had happened.

Aidan told his brother what had happened at the sweet shop. When he finished, Nicholas said the girl's words made no sense. She was wrong — Benevolence and the three servants were certainly alive — and he wondered why someone would concoct such a bizarre lie.

Nicholas continued, "I'll admit something odd's going on. For one thing, the servants haven't aged in a decade. I mentioned it to Mrs. Campbell last evening, but she changed the subject. You missed Father's funeral, but trust me, they appear much younger today than they did then. They're near ninety, but you'd never know it. Perhaps the fountain of youth is hidden somewhere on the estate."

Aidan said, "Come back to the village with me. Let's confront the girl and get an explanation."

As he eavesdropped, Barclay frowned. Whatever it took, he must keep them from returning to Torcall. Lady Dayne might think of something. She'd created this mess, after all. Over the strenuous objections of Cook, Mrs. Campbell and him, she'd insisted on enticing her children to come home for Christmas. If they did, Barclay had argued, it would be impossible to keep the secrets. As long as it was just them — plus Laris and John — no one would be the wiser. But Benevolence refused to listen. There was much at stake — everything, to be honest. Lady Dayne had seemed resigned, saying it was time. She called this the Last Christmas, and Barclay understood that assessment was likely correct.

Nicholas was talking now, suggesting they speak to Aidan's mother instead. From the moment they'd received invitations, everything about this trip had been a mystery. She should be providing the answers instead of some shopkeeper in the village.

Aidan disagreed. "Mother never cared for the townspeople. Perhaps she faked their deaths to keep people away from the castle. The girl — Ella was her name — she knows more than she told me. We must ask her, Nicky."

Just then the door opened and Benevolence swept into the room. "Welcome home, Aidan. I've met your…whatever Isabella is to you. Friend? Lover? It makes no difference. She came down for breakfast, announcing that you had gone for a walk to the village. You passed the great room a moment ago without even stopping to say hello to your mother. How inconsiderate."

She paused. "Aidan? What's the matter with you?"

Eyes wide and mouth agape, he stared at his mother, the person whom the shopkeeper declared had died a year ago in this castle. There she was, alive and apparently as healthy as they were.

"Mother," he stammered. "You…uh, you look good."

"What's wrong?" the old lady demanded, cursing herself for what she had allowed to happen. "You look as if you've seen a ghost. Tell me about your visit to the village. Did you speak to someone?"

She knows, Nicholas thought as he watched their interaction.

Aidan approached her, but Benevolence put up her hands and backed away. She also changed the subject.

"There's no call for meaningless displays of affection. It's enough for me that you came, as late as you were. Your 'friend' has already informed the family that if she hadn't bought the tickets, you wouldn't be here. I can't imagine where you found her, but I find her lack of social graces annoying."

"Give her a break, Mother," Aidan muttered. "You just met her."

"I'll give her a 'break,' as you quaintly put it, but what about you? You know better. You walk into my home, pass by the room where I sit, and sequester yourself here with Nicholas for a private conversation. What was so important? Did something happen in the village? You had no business going there."

"It's wonderful to see you too, Mother. For God's sake, I went to town. Why shouldn't I have? You'd think I committed murder. I'm thirty-nine years old. I'll go wherever I please. And leave Izzy out of this. She has enough issues without taking on this family's too." He shut his mouth, plopped down on the couch, and looked away for a moment before deciding he had nothing to lose by asking the question.

"What happened at Torcall Castle on Boxing Day last year?"

"I have no idea what you're talking about." She turned to leave.

"Don't walk out on me, Mother! I came a long way — yes, Izzy paid for it, but only after I promised to repay her — and I came because you invited me. I haven't seen you in twenty-three years. I put up with your and Father's overbearing ways and constant criticism until I was sixteen and refused to take it anymore. I'm the outcast of the family — that's no news to anyone — but you caused it. Now talk to me. A shopkeeper said you and the servants died here a year ago. Why would she tell me a story like that?"

THE LAST CHRISTMAS

She looked at him from across the room for what seemed like a long time. Then she spoke. "Barclay and the others were right. It *was* a mistake to bring everyone here — especially you. I had good intentions, and everything was fine for almost twenty-four hours. Until your arrival, Aidan."

"But things aren't fine," Nicholas said. "Our bedrooms are exactly as they were when we were children. I had a visitor last night — the man you suggested we ask about our scavenger hunt. Malcolm Dayne. He's the one who told me Aidan was at the front door, so I didn't dream it. You summoned us home. Now I want answers too."

She opened the door. "Come to the great room. Although you may regret asking, you'll get the answers you require."

CHAPTER TWENTY

There was an air of mystery as the family waited for her entrance. Everyone had been busy decorating when Barclay entered the room, advised them Lady Dayne had an important announcement, and asked them to find chairs and wait for her arrival. The servants entered the room and stood at the rear. Laris and John were in one corner and the older ones — Cook, Mrs. Campbell and Barclay — stood some distance away by the windows.

Benevolence swept into the room, her face a grim mask of something between fear and determination. She took her usual chair, looked at Nicholas, and spoke.

"The servants — not Laris and John, but the others — must be having quite the 'I told you so' moment right now. They strove without success to convince me that gathering you all here was a foolish and risky idea. There was no need for it; it was better to leave well enough alone; it would make no difference anyway — every shred of logic they came up with, I dismissed. But they were right. Geoffrey Dayne's offspring have their own lives, careers and families, in which this castle plays no part. Despite that fact, I had to make one valiant effort to avert what my husband — your father — considered the most tragic thing that could befall the Dayne family and its ancestral home."

Except for logs popping in the fire, there were no sounds in the room. No one spoke — all waited for details regarding her cryptic statement.

"The castle is cursed, thanks to Malcolm Dayne, our clan chief who hid Bonnie Prince Charlie here in 1746. Even now he roams the halls, protecting the family from evil."

"Give me a break," Poppy stage-whispered dramatically. "A curse and a ghost? What bullshit!"

"Silence!" came an enormous shout. The mighty roar permeated every inch of the room, echoing from wall to wall. A strong, gruff voice screamed the word again. "Silence!"

The room was abuzz with confusion, and at last Jill asked, "What on earth was that?"

Benevolence smiled. "Not something on earth, my dear granddaughter. And not what — who. *That* is who you heard." She pointed toward the back of the room.

There were gasps and cries as everyone turned to look. Standing near the door, dressed in a Dayne tartan kilt and wearing a green tam, was a man six and a half feet tall with a mustache and a long, unruly beard. He looked every inch the mighty warrior he had once been, and he floated just above the floor.

The staff looked nonchalant, as though his appearance was commonplace. Nicholas recognized him, of course. He and Malcolm Dayne had spoken last night in his bedroom.

"Come forward, Malcolm," Benevolence said, and the family members drew back as the huge man swept between their chairs to stand by her at the fireplace. She looked like a doll beside the tall, grizzled phantom.

"No one in the history of this clan has more fiercely protected it than this man," she began. "He fought in the battle of Culloden, hid the prince here, and watched from the shore as Charles left Scotland for the last time. He defended the castle when the Redcoats came to destroy it. Part of it lies in ruin today, but Malcolm's efforts saved half. Your grandfather many times removed, the third Earl of Torcall, named his brother the clan chief, and Malcolm swore an allegiance to the Dayne clan that remains to this day."

When she paused, the giant Scotsman spoke. "Aye, my kinsmen and women. Lady Dayne speaks the truth, and it would behoove you to heed the words. I love this clan with all my soul. I swore allegiance to it almost three hundred years ago, and to ensure future clan chiefs would do the same, I paid a wizard to put a hex on the castle. If for ten years no clan chief lives within these walls, the castle will fall into ruin and the Dayne clan will come to a tragic end."

An instant later, Malcolm Dayne vanished, leaving Benevolence standing alone before the astonished group. Everyone spoke at once; questions flew as the assemblage tried to understand what they were witnessing.

After a moment, she resumed where their ancestor had left off. "Your father, Geoffrey, may he rest in peace, died in this very room on the last day of the year 2010. That was nine years and three hundred fifty-nine days ago. On the day of his demise, Nicholas became the clan chief and eighth Earl of Torcall. But you have not lived in this house one day since his death. Until yesterday, you never returned in all those years. Nicholas, it should be clear now why I summoned you home. The future of your castle and your clan are in your hands."

"But why bring the others home if the curse involves only me — the clan chief?"

"None of you may believe me, but I wanted the family together one last time. I said there's money for each of you, and now you have a mystery to solve. Now that you're working as a team, each of you will enjoy the rewards should you succeed."

Tiona asked, "Enough about curses and clan chiefs. What's going on here, Mother? The bedrooms have become our childhood rooms. You and the servants seem to be in the peak of health — remarkably younger looking than nine years ago."

Aidan joined in. "The shopkeeper in the village claims you died on Boxing Day a year ago. The servants too.

She said everyone in town knows about it. What prompted such a preposterous claim? What are you trying to do here?"

That was news to everyone but Nicholas, and their cries and questions came as no surprise.

Benevolence stood stoically before them for so long that the awkward situation set the granddaughters to squirming. The adults shushed each other, and Jill meekly said, "Grandmother, are you going to answer Aidan? We all want to know."

"The story she told you is true."

Tiona wished for another Xanax, Noelle appeared to be in shock, and the children turned to look at the servants, three of whom stood like statues, their blank expressions revealing nothing. Laris and John seemed agitated, their eyes darting here and there as they avoided the family's stares.

Nicholas stood. "Quiet, everyone! Let her continue."

"The castle is old and drafty," she began. "As you know, of the hundred rooms that remain, less than twenty are habitable. Last year on Boxing Day, the morning after Christmas, I awoke shivering under the blankets. A hard freeze had come during the night, bringing temperatures to record lows for this part of northern Scotland. Laris and John were off in Mallaig to be with their families, so I asked Barclay to build an enormous fire in this fireplace beside which I'm standing. Mrs. Campbell, Cook, Barclay and I stayed here in the great room to keep warm.

"When lunchtime came, Cook put on a heavy coat and went to the kitchen to prepare things. I remarked that the dining room was unheated, and the roaring fire was no match for the chill that lingered in this room. Barclay remembered an old kerosene space heater in the basement that hadn't been used in years. He brought it up, got it going, and soon I felt comfortable for the first time that day. Mrs. Campbell set our lunch in here instead, over on that table." She paused and pointed. "Our undignified lunch in the great room would have appalled your father, but we had no choice."

Nicholas observed how the servants' faces lit up as they listened.

"I recall becoming drowsy as we ate, and I knew something was off when I saw Barclay drop his wineglass onto the floor. Dazed, he looked at it as if he didn't understand why it was there. I realized I was in the same state; I couldn't form words to comment. Within a few minutes we were all asleep, thanks to deadly carbon monoxide fumes issuing forth from the ancient space heater. Laris and John, bless their hearts, returned in the evening and found the four of us sitting around our improvised dining table, dead as doornails."

That was the last straw. Every family member jumped up, shouting, questioning, pointing and crying. Their confusion was understandable. The matriarch, mother to two in this room, stepmother to two more, and grandmother to three, had just revealed something that rational people couldn't comprehend. This was no zombie — she wasn't the walking dead or a mindless corpse. She was flesh and blood — or so she appeared as she stood before them conversing as always — but calmly stating the impossible. The woman speaking to them was dead. She'd said so herself.

Each wondered what they were. Phantoms? Corpses?

"Prove it, Benevolence," Noelle shouted.

She smiled and nodded. An instant later she, Mrs. Campbell, Cook and Barclay vanished.

CHAPTER TWENTY-ONE

Some held each other close, others babbled as they struggled to understand, and the three granddaughters sat together in a daze. As head of the family, Nicholas struggled to maintain his composure and take command of this unthinkable situation.

He summoned John and Laris to join him. They were uncomfortable standing in front of eight people they'd met only yesterday and who'd just learned ghosts inhabited their ancestral home. The young couple had also found it incomprehensible at first, but by now they were accustomed to the bizarre situation.

"Sit down, everyone," Nicholas said as he turned to Laris. "I assume Benevolence's story is true." The girl nodded, her eyes downcast and her hands shaking.

"When did you know?"

John answered in his thick brogue. "Everything seemed fine at first. We came here in the summer of 2018. We answered an ad seeking a live-in couple to be handyman and housekeeper. We had only worked one other place, and it sounded perfect. Your family's solicitor from Glasgow met us in Mallaig for the interview. A few days later he offered us the positions. We accepted and came to Torcall Castle for the first time. We met Lady Dayne and her staff, she explained our duties, and Barclay helped us get settled in the gatehouse."

Laris raised her head and spoke softly. "They seemed to like us, and we were happy here. Working in a six-hundred-year-old castle is something few people would ever experience, and we enjoyed our duties. Lady Dayne appreciated us and treated us well. She let Mrs. Campbell assign duties, and she was always nice to John and me. Everything went well until..." She choked back a sob, and John picked up the explanation.

"Things went well until Boxing Day last year," he said. "Things happened just as Lady Dayne told you. We were with my dad and mum in Mallaig over Christmas. We came back, dropped our bags at the gatehouse, and came down here to see if the mistress needed anything."

Laris said they unlocked the front door, stood in the silent hallway, and called out. No one answered. It was freezing in the house, the fires and space heater having long since burned out. They entered the great room, found four bodies slumped around a table filled with uneaten meals, and panicked. What could they do? There was no police officer in the tiny village, and Mallaig was eight miles away. Lady Dayne had spoken of children, but the servants knew neither their names nor how to contact them.

John continued. "Laris came up with the answer. We should contact the family solicitor in Glasgow — the man who had hired us. It being a holiday, the call would have to wait until the next morning, so we moved into the library." He paused and looked at Nicholas. "Begging your pardon, milord, but we sorely needed a drink. We entered the library, poured ourselves some brandy, and talked about what to do with the bodies."

Laris took his hand. "And that's when...well, that's when our lives changed forever. Things will never be the same for us, because of what happened that evening." She paused a moment and said, "Perhaps another wee drop of that brandy might be helpful now."

"Of course," Nicholas said. "Hold your thoughts." He left the room for several minutes and returned with the drink trolley. "I thought perhaps the rest of us might need one too," Nicholas explained, and the others appreciated it. After they had drinks, the couple continued.

They decided to leave things alone, lock up the house, and call the solicitor the next day. If he agreed, they would drive to the police station in Mallaig. John closed the liquor cabinet as Laris carried their glasses to the kitchen. Someone spoke; thinking it was Laris, he walked into the hall and said, "Do you need me?"

"No, everything's quite all right," came a voice from the great room. It wasn't Laris, although it could have been no one else, as they were the only two people in the house. The only two living people in the house, he corrected himself.

He walked into the great room and said, "Laris, are you here?" Instead of his wife, he faced a spectacle beyond belief.

"There they sat around the table, talking to each other, where they'd been dead a few minutes earlier," he explained as the family clung to every word of his fascinating story. "Lady Dayne looked up at me and said, 'John, you're back, I see. Would you ask Laris to help Mrs. Campbell clear these dishes? I'm afraid we didn't consume much of our lunches.'

"I was speechless, light-headed and about to faint. I croaked out a call for Laris, who came from the kitchen to see what I wanted. She screamed when Barclay stood as she entered the room. He always did that for a lady, but today he was dead, and it took us both by surprise.

"She half-fell into my arms, and Barclay helped me move her to the couch. Everything about him appeared just as it had been before, and I thought perhaps we'd hallucinated when we first came back to the house. Whisky wasn't to blame — I hadn't had a drop until a few minutes earlier. Both of us stammered and stuttered, trying to make some sense out of something that made no sense at all."

Laris looked toward the back of the room and smiled. The others turned to see that Benevolence and her three loyal servants had returned. They stood listening to the couple's retelling of a story in which everyone had played a role.

"Mother!" Tiona cried when she saw her, but Benevolence put a finger over her lips. To Laris she said, "Continue, please. I hadn't heard the account from your point of view, and I'm finding it fascinating."

"Thank you, ma'am," Laris said. "Well, like John said, we didn't know what to think. I wondered a moment if I were dreaming, but then Lady Dayne explained about the heater. It was difficult to grasp that I was speaking to a...a deceased person, but then she told us about the curse. Somehow she, Mrs. Campbell, Cook and Barclay received some kind of dispensation, I suppose, that allowed them to appear as living persons for one year. If she could entice the clan chief to take up residence in his ancestral home, she could break the curse."

She glanced to the back of the room. "I'm very uncomfortable speaking for you, milady," she said to Benevolence, who came forward to finish the narrative.

"John and Laris have been faithful and loyal helpmates during this past year," she said. "Sometimes it has been difficult adjusting to the reality that certain things we always assumed are not true. Death is not always as final as it's purported to be.

"Now that you know all this, I will answer some of your questions. Why did I insist you leave by sundown on Boxing Day? Because our one year expires then. I cannot say what will happen to the four of us at that time, but you must not be here. Why do your bedrooms appear as they were decades ago? That is a mystery to me as well. It happened at the same time we were 'awakened' from our slumber, and may have to do with the spirits enticing

Nicholas back to the castle by offering him a comfortable haven — his old bedroom as it was when he was a teen. That wasn't my doing, that's all I can say."

Nicholas said, "So all the fuss about our coming home for one last Christmas, gathering the family together and the like, all that was a lie, correct? There's no pot at the end of the rainbow that we all must find. There's no money to be distributed. You brought me here to save the clan and the castle, and you brought the others because it truly is your last Christmas."

"Always the cynic," his stepmother said, shaking her head. "You're wrong, Nicholas. I must explain more so you will fully understand why you're here. We've talked enough for now; I'll tell you more while we dine. Cook, hustle off to the kitchen and prepare lunch for us. Everyone else, I want this Christmas tree trimmed like it's the last one you'll ever see in this castle, because that may be precisely what it is."

CHAPTER TWENTY-TWO

The Dayne family finished decorating as their matriarch had instructed, although the frivolity, lightheartedness and laughter from earlier were missing now. This was to be no merry Christmas. The realization that nothing really was as it seemed, and the impending doom for the castle and clan, bore heavily on each of the Dayne children. What everyone had hoped would be a tolerable Christmas get-together was dashed. Now melancholy and gloom hung over the family.

As Mrs. Campbell, Barclay and Cook scurried about here and there, setting the table, preparing drinks and the luncheon, and handling their usual duties, Tiona went to her room. She took another Xanax and sat on her bed as tears streamed down her cheeks. They were a dysfunctional family, but no one deserved this. Not the children, not Benevolence, and not the servants old or new. Her mother was not a living being. She and the others appeared so, but they were mere specters, and Tiona's heart ached at what lay ahead.

Nicholas sat by his stepmother at the dining table and asked more about the curse she claimed would befall them in a few days. "All I have to do is technically live in the castle, is that right? Why can't I extend my trip perhaps two weeks, get us past December thirty-first and into the new year, and 'live' in the castle long enough to break the curse?"

"That's ridiculous. You're an intelligent man, Nicholas. Smart and crafty like your father, but you're no match for Malcolm Dayne. He understood what he was doing when he ordered that curse. If you want to argue or try to circumvent the rules, then speak with him yourself. All you need do is summon him and he will appear."

Everyone turned to listen as she tapped on her water glass with a spoon. "Now that you know my secret, there is more for you to learn. You trimmed the tree, and after lunch it should be back on the hunt for all of you. Malcolm will explain more about what you're looking for."

The old warlord appeared at the far end of the long, rectangular room. Although his feet didn't touch the floor, he strode toward them with a confident swagger and stopped at Benevolence's chair. He put his hand on her shoulder and said, "Something of immense value lies hidden on the Dayne estate. I had a part in selecting where it lies, and I swore an oath of secrecy as to its whereabouts. At the time I pledged to guard it, I failed to consider that the oath might someday put me at odds with a member of my own clan, a person who both deserves to know and who needs it. That person is you, Lord Dayne." He pointed at Nicholas.

"I've heard the tales about Jacobite treasure hidden somewhere in the Highlands," Nicholas said. "Is that what we're looking for?"

Malcolm smiled. "That it is, laddie."

"The estate has almost twenty thousand acres, Uncle. With just over forty-eight hours to find something you hid and cannot help us locate, we haven't a chance. I'm sure both you and Benevolence understand that. What's the purpose of giving us a futile exercise?"

"Because you *must* find it. The future of the Dayne clan hinges on your making use of it to save the castle and the dynasty. I cannot reveal the whereabouts, but listen closely to this story. The clues in it can help you."

He explained the Dayne clan's connection to the Jacobites. As staunch Catholics, they aligned themselves with Bonnie Prince Charlie and the rebels early on, and Malcolm stood erect and proud as he told them of his participation in the ill-fated battle of Culloden in April of 1746.

"A thousand brave men died on that field," he said, removing his tam and holding it over his heart. "I lost many a friend and relative that day, but God spared me because my work wasn't finished. Four of us helped the prince escape the Redcoats and brought him here to the castle. I gave him refuge in the Queen's Tower, and he hid there for several days until the English began searching house-to-house for him. They were moving from one estate to the next, and we learned they would be at Torcall Castle soon. My friends took him northward, always staying a step or two ahead of the damned Redcoats.

"For a time he evaded his pursuers, but at last it became clear our mission had failed. The Stuart dynasty would not be restored to the British throne. He returned to Torcall Castle one last time, stayed the night nearby, and one bright September morning four months after the battle, his most loyal followers — myself included — stood on the shore and bade him Godspeed as he left Scotland forever."

The rugged warrior brushed away a tear. "Although he would never be king, to his followers Charles was a royal equal to Mary, Queen of Scots, who also visited and overnighted within these walls. You learned that a clock was added to the tower after Queen Mary stayed. That room — the clock room at the apex of the tower — is where I hid the prince. The clock is crucial to your efforts, Nicholas. Find it, understand it, and you will be successful."

"I'm going to read the clues again to refresh our memories," Tiona said.

I watched each of you grow, although I held my tongue about what I saw.

Numbers are very important to me.
I am older than anyone living today.
I have seen wars, rebellions, royalty and treasure.
Although I often communicated, I never spoke.
Mary and Charles are names of great significance.
I hold a secret of immense value.
Who or what am I?

Nicholas asked Malcolm how his father could have written these clues without knowing what the prize was or where it was hidden.

"Because I told him the words to write. I know both the prize and its location."

"Why are you doing this? You put a curse on the castle and the clan, but now you want to help us solve Benevolence's riddle? How are those two things related?"

"Your stepmother already explained it to you. There must be a laird — a clan chief — living in the castle. That was a condition of my pact with the devil long ago that saved this place from the Redcoats. You're the last hope. Good luck."

With that, he and Benevolence disappeared.

CHAPTER TWENTY-THREE

Noelle said, "Jesus, I don't think I can take many more revelations. All this about their deaths — everything is true, right, Nicky? It must be, with all the appearing and disappearing, but what's going on?"

"They're still here because the clan faces extinction in a few years. At sixty-seven and with no male heirs, I'm the last of the clan chiefs. I'll deal with that later, because we have little time remaining. It's two o'clock on Christmas Eve. That gives us two days and four hours to solve the puzzle and claim...whatever. We must put aside time to celebrate Christmas with Benevolence, presuming she returns, so each hour that remains is precious."

The dazed, puzzled expressions on everyone's faces were understandable, given the revelations of the past two hours that upended traditional beliefs in life and death. Nicholas summoned Laris and John to his side and said, "We are in your debt. You found yourselves involved in something beyond one's imagination. You joined three elderly servants and an old woman, and last Christmas you became the only living souls within these walls."

"Yes, milord," John said. "To be honest, it scared us both very much at first. Every child hears his share of eerie ghost stories, but last Christmas everything we believed — or didn't — about ghosts flew out the bloody window. The stories are real — *they're* real. But they died, like Lady Dayne said."

"Can you give us anything else before we continue searching? The secret about the clock in the tower, for instance?"

Laris said, "We never heard there was a clock there, but since the top part is just a pile of rubble, something might be buried inside, I guess."

Nicholas dismissed them and got the Dayne family history book from the library. Seeking entries that might provide a clue to the clock, he flipped through the pages covering the late eighteenth century. He stopped in 1798 when he saw an entry about improvements in the village of Torcall. The tiny town had sprung up in the fourteen hundreds when the castle was constructed; the earl at the time hired men to erect houses and shops for the laborers and workers who were building Torcall Castle and tending to the vast estate. In due course families grew, more stores opened, and within twenty years it was a thriving hamlet with a Saturday market, a church with services every other Sunday led by an itinerant priest, and over two hundred worshippers.

From medieval times there had been a town square, and after the queen's visit in 1564, the earl erected a statue in her honor. Today the life-sized bronze stood on a square black base four feet high that elevated the monarch to a lofty place of honor. Nicholas and his siblings recalled it easily; they'd spent untold hours in the village as privileged children of the earl, a man whom the villagers loved and respected.

As Nicholas read random passages aloud, Noelle interrupted. "Time's a-wastin'. As you said, we have two days and four hours. Ticktock, brother. I say let's go back to the tower and look for the clock."

"Hold on," he said. "Here's something interesting." He read for a moment longer. "Did anyone know the church in the village was struck by lightning in 1898? It burned to the ground, and the earl built a new one."

THE LAST CHRISTMAS

Tiona asked Nicky why he was going off on a tangent. They were trying to solve a puzzle, not get a history lesson. The others murmured in assent.

Without replying, he continued reading for a moment, paused, and said, "Listen to this entry written by the earl that same year, 1898. 'By the time the church was destroyed, more than a hundred people attended services. My family and I often joined them, and the tiny nave couldn't accommodate the parishioners, who resorted to taking turns which Sunday to attend.

"'The village needed a bigger church, and the fire that consumed the old one was God's sign that I needed to deal with the issue. An architect from Inverness designed a much larger stone building, and I assigned forty laborers to the project. They completed it just before the dawn of the new century, in November 1899.'"

"Nicky, stop it, for God's sake!" Noelle stood and said she was going to the tower. Anyone who wished could come along and skip the rest of the lesson. Aidan and Tiona stood with her, and the grandchildren went along too. They had all reached the back of the room and were moving toward the hall when Nicholas, who besides Carly was the only one left, began reading aloud.

"As the spire of our new church rose into the sky, I decided a clock would be a fine addition. I remembered where I could get a grand one, the clock that had graced the Queen's Tower. It had lain in the rubble since the English destroyed the tower in 1746. Was it possible the clock still worked? A skilled clockmaker from Glasgow came and repaired it, and soon it was as good as new. My laborers created a place in the steeple for the huge old clock, and the townspeople thought it was splendid."

Nicholas closed the book and stood. "Our clock is in the church steeple. There's no use looking here. It's time to go to the village." He asked John for the keys to the Rolls and drove them to town.

They stood in the square with Mary's statue behind them and gazed at the spire of the old stone church. Each of them had seen the clock countless times over the years, but no one gave it a thought, even now when it seemed a clock was the clue they sought. As it was Christmas Eve, the building was unlocked, and ladies inside were decorating the nave for services this evening and tomorrow. Nicholas introduced himself and the others, said they wanted to look at the clock, and one of the ladies showed them a door behind which lay a narrow circular staircase leading to the clock room. Nicholas started first, and at the top he pushed open a trapdoor, stepping into a small round room that barely held the eight of them.

Noelle clapped her hands, and pigeons roosting high above flew away through an opening that had once been a window. The huge round clock took up one entire wall; a door beside it opened outside, allowing access to the dial in case the hands needed adjusting. Jill opened the door and gasped as she saw it led onto a very narrow walkway thirty feet above the square.

"I hope to God the clue isn't on the front of the clock," she said as she closed the door. "Someone else can go out there and find out."

In the cramped space, they examined the back of the clock. Its mechanism was in the middle of a huge metal circle marked by rust stains and pigeon droppings. No one had thought to bring gloves, and none relished using their fingers to brush away the acrid dung. They held their breaths against the overpowering stench of ammonia.

They took a break after examining every square inch of the metal surface up as high as they could reach. But much more of the clock remained above them, and Noelle thought she might see faint writing near the mechanism in the middle.

"I wish we had a ladder," he said, and Aidan volunteered to go downstairs and see if the ladies might have one. Soon he lumbered back up the stairs, the bang-banging sounds a sign he had found what he needed. He also had brought damp cloths for removing the bird droppings.

Two of them held the rickety ladder while Nicholas climbed it. He used the light from his phone to examine the area Noelle had seen, and he said it did indeed look like writing. Like the rest of the clock, it was encrusted in grime, but when he tried the damp rag, the letters faded away. He used his fingernails to pick off poop, rubbed away dust with his hand, and at last he read words.

"It's a series of sentences," he called down to the others. "Very faint and almost faded away, but still visible. I'll take a picture." He steadied himself on the ladder, held his phone close, and shot several photos, some with flash and some without.

He climbed down and expanded the shots. Although difficult to make out, they were words.

"One day…a Queen to…to Torcall came." That was the first line.

"That's Mary, right?" Steph asked, and Nicholas said she was the only queen who visited the castle or the village.

"The next line reads, 'And laid her head to rest.' Can someone write this down?"

"I'm on it," Tiona said. "I'm putting the words in my phone as you read."

"Here goes two more. 'In Mary's name two monuments' — that's one line — 'Her visit here attest.' That's the next one."

Tiona read, "'One day a Queen to Torcall came, And laid her head to rest. In Mary's name two monuments, Her visit here attest.' It's a poem."

"Two monuments. What are they?" Poppy asked, and her mother said perhaps the Queen's Tower at the castle and the statue in the square down below.

"I see two more stanzas," Nicholas said. "Four lines each and easier to read. Here we go. 'He falls from grace who would be king, And leaves behind his land. His rebel band must hide the spoils, From England's ruthless hand.' That seems straightforward. Bonnie Prince Charlie should have been king, according to the Jacobites who supported him. He has to leave Scotland forever, and — here's where things get interesting — his men, his 'rebel band,' must hide the spoils from the English."

The granddaughters chattered away all at once.

"Is that what we're looking for?"

"What are spoils? Does that mean money?"

"It sounds like something's hidden. Maybe it's in the church."

Nicholas said, "Let's read the last four lines before we go jumping to conclusions. Jill, spoils are things you take from someone else. It might be money or something else of value. Poppy, I hope what we're after wasn't hidden in the church, because it burned to the ground, as you'll recall."

He began to read, laboriously mouthing out each dusty, grimy word until Tiona got the sentences down. Then she read them as a stanza.

May Charles now join that noble Queen,
Forever linked as one.
She guards what Jacobites have hid
For Scotland's bravest Son.

"Is that it?" Noelle asked, and when Nicholas nodded, she said, "Then let's get the hell out of here. The stench is making me nauseous."

They climbed down the decaying staircase and emerged into the nave, where wreaths, paper bells and trumpets, and sprigs of holly had transformed the austere, stone-walled room into a festive scene. They thanked the church women, said goodbye, and drove back to the castle.

CHAPTER TWENTY-FOUR

Barclay stood in the hallway as they walked back into Torcall Castle. As a phantom who seemed as real as they, the family felt uneasy for a moment.

"Any success on your trip to the village?" Barclay asked, and Nicholas said it appeared his father's clues from nine years ago led them to the church. He described the words they'd found.

"Who would have written those words, and when?" Aidan asked. "The clock stood in the tower from when Mary visited in the mid-fifteen hundreds until the Redcoats destroyed it around 1746. It lay in the rubble from then until one of our ancestors plucked it out, had it repaired, and installed it in the church steeple in 1898. Someone scrawled a poem on the back of the clock, but why and when?"

"I beg your pardon, milord," Barclay said, "but I have an idea. The prince occupied the clock tower before escaping Scotland. He slept in the clock room itself. Perhaps he wrote the words."

Nicholas jerked his head up. "That reminds me of something. I remember seeing initials at the bottom of that poem." He pulled up the pictures on his phone. "Look at those two small letters below the last line. Can you make them out? Looks like an *M* and a *D*."

"So it's not Prince Charles Edward Stuart," Noelle said.

"Malcolm Dayne, perhaps?" Aidan suggested, and Nicholas nodded.

"That's possible. The prince wouldn't have written words about his own departure, which hadn't happened yet. Someone else wrote the poem after Charles left our castle. Malcolm's my guess too, although I don't see that old reprobate waxing poetic on us."

Benevolence – another ghost in their midst -- sat in the great room as the family filed in and greeted her with uneasy smiles. Mrs. Campbell and Laris wheeled in the trolley and prepared Christmas Eve cocktails.

"Did you have success this afternoon?" Benevolence asked as Nicholas stood by the fire near her chair. Yes, he told her, it appeared his father's enigmatic clues referred to the clock in the church steeple. They found writing on the back — a cryptic poem that might be significant.

Jill confronted her grandmother. "I'm not sure how all this ghost stuff works," she said, "but you know the secret thing we're looking for, so why can't you just tell us? The curse keeps that old man Malcolm from helping us, but not you. Spill the beans, Grandmother."

Benevolence smiled. "It isn't that easy. I don't understand your father's clues, nor have I ever given it much thought, since the quest wasn't mine. I'm not the heir to the clan — Nicholas is. My only concern was getting all of you back here for the last Christmas and a chance to break the curse. Now please tell me what the poem you found says."

She listened closely as Tiona read the lines aloud once again, and she sat silently as the servants dispensed cocktails. "Go on with celebrating," she said. "I want to ponder the meaning."

The girls walked over to the tree and looked through the few presents beneath it. Each of them had brought a small gift for the others, plus some for Benevolence, although it seemed silly now to be giving presents to a ghost.

They realized Malcolm Dayne had joined them when someone saw his shadowy figure in a dark corner and pointed him out. He strode to the fireplace and said, "Where do you go from here, Nicholas? As laird, it's your responsibility to lead the others."

"You wrote the poem, didn't you? It mentions two monuments in Mary's name. Those are the Queen's Tower and the statue in the village square. Am I getting warm?"

The old warrior's face bore a puzzled look. "Are you too warm? Perhaps you should move away from the fire."

Several people laughed as Nicholas explained that the phrase was an American saying. "Am I going in the right direction?" he asked instead, and Malcolm repeated that he couldn't help them.

"I wrote those words," he admitted. "The clock lay among the ruins of the tower, thanks to the bloody Redcoats. It was too massive to throw away, so I wrote those lines in hopes someone would find them. I'm surprised it took over two hundred years."

Tiona said, "Uncle Malcolm, let me try to phrase a question that you can answer. The first stanza of the poem must refer to Mary. She came to Torcall, 'laid her head to rest' by overnighting here, and two monuments mark her visit — the tower our ancestor built in her name and the statue. Are those statements correct?"

"They are," he said with the slightest of smiles. "I may not interpret them or guide you, but I can attest to the accuracy of a statement." Tiona smiled and thanked him for confirming they had deciphered the first stanza.

They picked apart the second stanza of four lines. The one who "would be king" fell from grace and had to leave his land. That seemed an obvious reference to Charles Stuart, whose rebel band had to hide "spoils" from the English.

Every Scottish child heard the mysterious legend of lost Jacobite gold hidden somewhere in the Highlands. In

1746 near Fort William, two French ships laden with supplies and bags of gold coins to support Prince Charles and his followers arrived. They came too late; the Battle of Culloden was over, and the Jacobites were on the run in the Highlands.

As Charlie stayed one step ahead of the English, the gold went from one clan chief to another, eventually ending up with Euan MacPherson at the time Prince Charles fled Scotland. Sometime later the prince sent his supporter Archibald Cameron to Scotland to find and secure the gold, but Cameron was betrayed and hung before completing his mission.

The bonnie prince never got his hands on the gold, and as years passed, rumors abounded as to its whereabouts. Most of them put it around Fort William, and stories cropped up of men finding gold, but the Jacobite treasure remained hidden.

Today, as the Dayne children and grandchildren sat around the great room with two specters, Nicholas grilled his ancestor. Malcolm couldn't interpret or guide, but Nicholas wondered if he might answer simple yes-or-no questions. As both a staunch supporter of Prince Charles and the clan chief who sheltered him, Malcolm surely had knowledge he hadn't revealed.

"Uncle," he began, "the poem refers to hidden spoils. Are those spoils the lost Jacobite gold?"

The enormous man stroked his beard for a moment, considering whether his answer would violate the pact, and nodded his head.

The others realized their brother was onto something. "Thank you. Rumor has it they hid the gold somewhere near Fort William. Can you tell me if that rumor is true?"

"I cannot guide you…" Malcolm replied, but Nicholas countered, saying all he asked was if the rumor was factual, not where the gold lay."

The old warrior smiled. "Clever, milord. I suppose there's no harm in answering that question. Yes, that's a fact."

Damn. Nicholas had hoped for a different answer. Fort William was fifty miles away. Did Malcolm write a poem on the clock about a horde of gold a day's ride from here? Implausible, but not impossible.

"Uncle, if the gold is hidden near Fort William…"

The man bellowed a laugh that echoed throughout the cavernous room. He bent double with laughter before regaining his composure.

With a wink, he said, "Caught you at your own game, my boy. How crafty you consider yourself, asking questions a certain way so I can answer them. Consider carefully what you asked, and what I answered."

"I asked you if they hid the gold…no, wait. I asked if the *rumor* that they hid the gold near Fort William was true."

"Aye, that you did. And I answered. I told you yes, that rumor is true."

"So we have forty-eight hours to find something that might be hidden anywhere within miles of Fort William. That's impossible…"

"And you're still not thinking," the warrior said.

Suddenly Poppy cried, "Uncle, is the gold still hidden near Fort William?"

He raised his eyebrows, pointed a finger at her, and said, "There's a smart lass. Keep thinking, for I cannot guide you." He crossed his arms in front of his massive girth and waited.

Poppy looked at Nicholas. "You asked if the gold was hidden near Fort William, and Malcolm said yes. They hid it there at first, but it doesn't mean it's still there. He can't guide us, so he won't confirm that it is somewhere else."

Nicholas looked at Malcolm, who grinned and winked. "There's a smart lass for sure," he said.

"I'm not certain how much we learned from that exercise," Nicholas commented as he asked Tiona to read the last four lines of the poem.

CHAPTER TWENTY-FIVE

May Charles now join that noble Queen,
Forever linked as one.
She guards what Jacobites have hid
For Scotland's bravest Son.

After Tiona read the words aloud, Nicholas commented they seemed the most enigmatic, and he asked if anyone had an idea what they meant.

"He should have been king," Steph suggested. "He's linked to Queen Mary because he was royalty too." She looked over at Malcolm and said, "I'm guessing you considered Charles Scotland's bravest son. You were a loyal Jacobite, and you hid him from the English. Am I right?"

He put his hand over his heart, bowed his head, and said, "There was none so brave as the bonnie prince."

Malcolm beamed with delight as he listened to the exchange, observing how close to the truth they came, only to veer off in the wrong direction. He desperately wanted to help; this was the most important task he had faced since he fought the Redcoats. As much as he wanted to help, he could not answer their critical questions, but they realized how that an indirect approach might work.

Nicholas asked for opinions about the third line, *She guards what Jacobites have hid*. The "she" doubtless referred to Mary, but she died centuries before Bonnie Prince Charlie was born. How could she guard what the Jacobites hid?

"I'd say it's a metaphor," Noelle suggested. "She couldn't literally guard treasure."

"Why not?" Aidan asked. "Where's she buried? Maybe someone hid it in her tomb."

"She's interred in Westminster Abbey in London. That's the last place it would be. The Jacobites wouldn't risk certain death by sneaking into England and depositing bags of French coins into her coffin. That makes no sense."

For several minutes they tossed out ideas until Nicholas called them to order. "Noelle's suggestion about the metaphor is a good one," he said. "If Mary's 'guarding' treasure, what might it mean?"

Jill blurted, "How about the Queen's Tower? It bears her name, and maybe she guards the treasure that's hidden inside."

"Good try, but you're wrong," Poppy said. "The dates don't fit. The English destroyed the tower after Prince Charles stayed here. He was on the run when the gold arrived, but the tower was already demolished. I doubt they hid gold in the ruins."

Nicholas agreed, but something nagged at his brain. Besides the Queen's Tower, there was the statue dedicated to Mary — likely the "second monument" mentioned in the poem — that stood in the village square. Which direction did the statue face? He wasn't sure, he didn't feel like driving to town to find out, and he asked the others.

Most recalled that Mary faced eastward, towards the church.

"Okay," he said. "Here's an idea. Mary guards what the Jacobites hid. She faces the church so she can watch over the treasure that's hidden inside."

Nicholas had more supposition to offer. The church dated back to the fourteen hundreds. The Dayne clan chief erected a statue after Mary's visit in 1564, and it faced the church. Around 1746, bags of French gold got passed from clan to clan, perhaps ending up in the hands of the Dayne clan chief. He chose the church to hide the treasure, where it stayed for centuries. The church burned in 1898. The gold wouldn't burn up, but we found no record of it turning up when the new church was erected. What if it was still there today?

Aidan said, "Presuming it was ever there, and if no one found it in 1898 — and those are two big ifs — then I'd say it had to be buried in the ground beneath the old church. Was the new church erected exactly where the old one stood? If so, we'd have to remove the stone floor block by block to find the treasure, which might not be there at all. Your theory has merit, but without demolishing the church, we can't prove it."

Noelle looked across the room to where Malcolm stood next to her stepmother. "How close are we?" she asked. "Are any of these deductions correct?"

"I cannot say."

"Here's one you can answer," Nicholas said. "Is the new church built exactly where the old one stood?"

"A good question, given the conversation you've been having. Yes, milord. Yes, on the same spot."

"Then I was right," Aidan said. "Something's buried under the stone floor."

The old man smiled but said nothing.

Tiona mentioned the cemetery next to the church which had hundreds of gravestones marking the final resting places of villagers who had served the Daynes. Perhaps the gold lay in the graveyard, its hiding place marked by a stone.

Benevolence interrupted them. "It's Christmas Eve and night has fallen. Let your ideas go for tonight. Other than gathering for lunch and a gift exchange tomorrow, you may use the remaining time to test your theories."

They refreshed their drinks, coaxed Steph into playing carols on the piano while others sang, and across the room Benevolence whispered to Malcolm, asking if they were on the right track.

"About the churchyard?" She nodded.

The old warrior said, "I suppose I can tell you. I can't help them, but you're not on the hunt." He revealed the secret and added, "I hope they don't waste too much of what little time remains. Only two days from this moment remain to solve the mystery."

CHAPTER TWENTY-SIX

Christmas Morning

Last night they had agreed to meet at sunrise — half past seven — to go to the village. There were gripes and grumbles from the night owls, but Nicholas ensured everyone had a steaming cup of tea or coffee, and this time they hiked the coastal trail to Torcall Village. The air was dry and fresh, and there was a light dusting of snow on the rutted lane and the craggy land around them. The temperature was in the low thirties, and as the eight Daynes walked, their breath made little clouds.

"One forgets how incredibly beautiful it is," Noelle remarked as waves crashed upon the rocks far below them. Across the waters of the Sound of Sleat they saw the hills of the Isle of Skye, and ahead, at the end of the trail, plumes of smoke from a hundred chimneys came into view.

"Merry Christmas! Good tidings to you!" came the greetings from the few people they passed along the way, early risers like themselves who were availing themselves of a quiet walk before the pandemonium of Christmas Day struck.

They entered the village and walked to the square, remarking on how beautiful the tree looked this year. There was just enough snow on its branches to give it a holiday feeling without covering the decorations the villagers had hung there.

The plan was to divide the cemetery among the eight of them. In a short time, they could examine each headstone. If one looked unusual, its location would be noted and a picture taken so they could return to it later.

Mary's statue stood resolute, facing east as some had remembered, and the few villagers who were out wondered why eight people were inspecting the graveyard. The search took just an hour, and after the hike back, everyone appreciated the warmth of the great room's hearth and was ready for another cup of coffee or tea.

Malcolm watched them file in and stamp their feet to dislodge the snow, and he listened to what they found in the village. They examined every marker but saw no clue that the gold might be in the cemetery.

The old man frowned. They were wasting what precious time remained. Were they up to the challenge? More importantly, would Nicholas Dayne agree to move to Scotland and occupy the castle as laird and clan chief? Would he do his duty and break the curse, or would the long, fateful history of Torcall Castle come to an ignominious end regardless of whether they found what they sought?

Even if Nicholas agreed to move back, Malcolm knew it was only a temporary solution. The man was sixty-seven and had two daughters. Without a son, the dynasty would end anyway upon his death. Malcolm's efforts would do nothing more than prolong the inevitable, but he hoped something unforeseen might happen to make things right.

"I think we should search inside the church," Nicholas was saying, and the others reminded him this was Christmas Day. A sign outside had announced that there would be three celebrations of Mass today, and although it was his prerogative as earl to poke around during services, it would be discourteous to interrupt worship on Christmas.

"We have tomorrow," Tiona said. "We can tackle the church then. This afternoon let's get a key from the priest so we can go inside first thing in the morning."

"That's pushing our luck. We have to solve the riddle and leave by six o'clock tomorrow afternoon. I say we look around the church today between services."

Tiona snapped, "Go for it. I haven't been to Mass in years, and I'm not going on Christmas Day. That's my choice, but I damned sure won't barge in and intrude on others who are there. Every person in the village will be at one of those services with families in tow. People will see you there, even if it's between services. You can be the insensitive lord of the manor, but count me out."

"I agree," Noelle said. "I'm with you, Tiona — Catholic in name only these days, but I respect this holy day."

They all looked up when Malcolm's voice resounded, "They're right, milord. Concentrate on other things today. If the church remains important, go there early tomorrow."

Nicholas asked if he was giving them a hint — a clue that the church wasn't worth their while.

Malcolm shook his head. "I cannot guide you on your quest. Today is a holy day. Respect the parishioners who want to worship and praise God on Christmas."

"What do we do now?" Noelle asked her ancestor, and Benevolence answered from her chair by the fire.

"We open our gifts and have Christmas lunch." The staff joined the family in the great room, Laris distributed flutes of champagne, and Nicholas asked them to gather around the Christmas tree for a picture.

"Be this the last Christmas or not, it's a time worth memorializing," he added, and he thought he saw a tiny smirk from his stepmother as she and the others took their places and Nicholas's iPhone snapped a delayed photo.

As was the tradition, the youngest members of the family — the granddaughters — passed out the presents everyone had brought. Nicholas had prepared envelopes for Barclay and the other servants, each containing a thousand pounds sterling, but it was ludicrous to give tangible gifts to people they now knew weren't alive. His largesse and thanks therefore were bestowed only on Laris and her husband, who much appreciated the gifts.

Christmas lunch reminded them of the old days. Noelle quipped that Cook was the finest deceased chef in all of Scotland, and the others laughed, uneasy at the odd situation they were in. If lunch yesterday had seemed enormous, today's holiday meal was beyond belief. This was a Christmas feast in true Dayne tradition, Nicholas commented.

The servants brought in course after course, each paired with a different wine Barclay expertly chose. There was an enormous turkey, countless side dishes, homemade bread, and the family's traditional dessert — Cook's delicious holiday cranachan made with cream, a bit of whisky, and fresh raspberries that Benevolence somehow managed to find even in the winter.

There was laughter and conversation throughout lunch. Tiona commented that at last it felt as if she had come home again. The feast and the fellowship elicited lots of stories of the old days, many fond memories, and even a tear or two. Malcolm observed their interaction from his honorary chair at the far end of the table. He did not eat, but it pleased him to see his clansmen and women enjoying themselves at home on this special day.

"Your father would have had his cigar and brandy now," Benevolence said as the last plates were cleared. "Christmas was the only day of the year when he performed that ritual at lunch instead of dinner."

Nicholas proclaimed himself as stuffed as the turkey had been and said he'd perform that ritual again tonight after dinner. "If there were time, I'd take a nap," he proclaimed, and the others agreed it would be nice, but they must keep on the quest.

THE LAST CHRISTMAS

"It's time for a strategy session," Noelle said, and the family — Benevolence and Malcolm included — gathered in the great room. Nicholas asked Tiona to read the poem once again to refresh everyone's minds, and when she finished, he asked if anyone could suggest where to look next.

Aidan said, "It's hard to believe considering the number of calories I just consumed, my brain seems to still be working. I have an idea."

CHAPTER TWENTY-SEVEN

"What if the last stanza of the poem involves neither the castle nor the village?" Aidan began. "The first stanza seems straightforward enough. It's about Mary's visit to Torcall Castle and mentions two monuments that attest to that event. We agree that those monuments are likely the Queen's Tower and the statue.

"The middle four lines seem to be about Bonnie Prince Charlie. He would have been king, and he left his land. According to legend, the French sent gold that arrived too late to help the Jacobite cause, and to keep it out of English hands, it was passed from clan to clan. Is everyone good with my logic so far?"

Everyone agreed Aidan's interpretation of those stanzas seemed correct.

"Okay, what if the third stanza isn't about the Dayne estate at all? It says Charles and the queen are linked forever somehow, and she guards what may be the French gold, doing so 'for Scotland's bravest Son,' which sounds like Prince Charles. The lines say nothing about what that link is or where she's standing guard. The treasure could be anywhere in Scotland that has a statue of Queen Mary. When she came to Torcall in 1564, I assume this wasn't the only castle she visited."

"You're right, if memory serves me," Nicholas answered. "She was on a grand tour, and she stayed several places. Malcolm, am I right?"

"You are, milord. Several castles in the Highlands were on her itinerary."

"Bad news for us," Noelle said, looking at her watch. "We have twenty-seven hours to find the answer, and no time to go castle-hopping."

Nicholas looked at his stepmother and said, "Benevolence, it seems to me the important issue here is the future of the castle and the clan. Malcolm's curse goes into effect on New Year's Eve at midnight. That's six days from now. Tell me why exactly are we scurrying around looking for a million quid of something that has nothing to do with my requirement to live here at Torcall Castle? Shouldn't you spend the brief time remaining on enticing me to move back to Scotland?"

"It's part and parcel of the same plan," she answered. "Stay the course and it will become clear to you."

Malcolm looked into her eyes and whispered, "My dear, I cannot help them, but you can. Time is short, the quest is critical, and I give you permission to tell them more."

Nicholas asked what he was talking about, but the warrior was silent. In a moment, Benevolence spoke.

"Nicholas, I hoped you all might get further on your own, and given more time, you might have done so. I can offer you one last thing to consider. Mary's statue stands in the village. At one time there was a plaque affixed to the base, but today it is gone. That plaque exists; find it and you will learn more."

"Talk about a needle in a haystack," Noelle muttered. "Twenty thousand acres on the estate, including an entire damned village, and all we have to do is find a lost plaque. I think we were better off not being tossed another crumb to add to an already unsolvable mystery."

Lost in thought, Nicholas ignored the others until someone asked what he was doing. He was considering how to pose questions that Malcolm could answer — ways he could help without breaking his oath.

"Uncle," he said at last, "I would like you to confirm the accuracy of two statements. First, the base under Mary's statue was not there originally. It was added later. Is that correct?"

"Aye."

"Second, the missing plaque will tell us where the gold is hidden. Am I right?"

Malcolm smiled. "No, laddie. You're *warm*, as you described yourself earlier. But you're not warm enough! You are using an incorrect word to describe the plaque."

"Incorrect? What did I say?"

Aidan interjected, "You called it a missing plaque."

Tiona said, "Mother said the plaque hadn't been on the base for a long time, but she didn't say it was missing."

Nicholas shrugged. "Lost, missing, misplaced, gone — different words for the same thing. The plaque isn't where it used to be, and now it's another thing we're supposed to find. If we do — what were the words you used, Benevolence? — we will 'learn more.' I'm getting fed up with all this secrecy. The closer we get to the deadline, which I also don't understand, by the way, the more things you add to the equation. We're almost out of time, I'm running low on patience, and I'm very close to saying to hell with it, I'm going home tomorrow and forgetting this Christmas ever happened."

"Nicky, what are you doing?" Carly cried. "Why can't you play along?"

"Because I'm too damned old for games. We all are. We're running around like toddlers playing hide-and-seek. Let me reveal a secret of my own. I've got a life and a career and a family. I'm happy living in Manhattan, and I am not — get this, everyone — I am *not* moving to Scotland to live in an ancient castle and play lord of the manor. Curse or no curse, dead people who've come to life to save the clan, the entire thing be damned. This is the twenty-first century, and I refuse to step back into the Middle Ages."

Nicholas stormed out of the room, slamming the door behind him. For a time, the only sounds were logs crackling in the fireplace as the family, Benevolence, and Uncle Malcolm pondered the consequences of his outburst.

At last Aidan spoke. "We need to keep trying. Mother brought us all home, and I intend to continue the search. Does anyone else want to quit?"

No one did. A few pointed out there was little else to do, the girls thought trying to solve a mystery was fun, and Noelle reminded them that the clock was still ticking and it would be dark in two hours. That would put an end to any outdoor searching that they should do today.

"Let's go back to the village," Tiona suggested. "Maybe we're missing something that's right before our eyes."

Noelle, the one most familiar with driving on the left side of the road, took the wheel of the Rolls, and in Torcall Village they found the square teeming with townspeople. The three o'clock Mass had just finished, and worshippers filed out of the church. When they saw the Rolls, several came over to meet the Dayne family and to wish them Merry Christmas. A few offered condolences for their mother's untimely death, in answer to which Poppy muttered under her breath, "When I left a minute ago, she didn't look too dead to me." Noelle gave her a jab in the ribs and told her to hush.

They examined all four sides of the statue's base, and Steph was the first to notice the holes where four screws had held the plaque. The others gathered to look, and an old man who was walking past saw them and came over.

"It's been gone a long time," he said.

"The plaque? Do you know where it is?"

"I couldn't say for certain, but some say it's in the castle. You're the Daynes, aren't you? Should be easy for you to find it!"

"Do you know what the plaque said?"

"I saw it when I was a lad, but that was sixty years ago. The mind doesn't work like it once did. But I remember one thing. It spoke of Bonnie Prince Charlie, God rest his soul. They put that base under Mary's statue not long after the Battle of Culloden, and it was to honor the prince . My father told me it made him proud. Two royals who had visited Torcall Village, now forever linked as one."

"Forever linked as one?" Noelle exclaimed. "Are those words on the plaque?"

"Maybe. My mind's a little slow, as I said. But I recall those words, so maybe they are."

Those same words were part of the poem on the clock. "Now we're getting somewhere," Tiona said as they returned to the castle to consider what was next.

CHAPTER TWENTY-EIGHT

They found Nicholas in the library, sitting by the fire with Benevolence and getting a head start on cocktail hour. He apologized for his earlier outburst but reiterated that he was leaving by six p.m. tomorrow, as Benevolence had insisted for all of them. His family would overnight in Glasgow and be in New York the next evening.

Aidan related their conversation with the old man in town, and he asked his mother if she knew where the plaque was.

She replied, "If everything's handed to you, then you lose the satisfaction of unraveling the mystery yourselves."

Carly said, "Nicky, at least help us. You may not need your share of a million pounds as much as the others, but I'll take it if you don't want it." The others laughed as he agreed to stay in the game, asking which of the castle's hundred extant rooms they should explore first.

"With eight of us, we can take twelve rooms each and make quick work of it," Aidan suggested, and it was a good idea except that the sun would set within the hour. Only twenty rooms were in use nowadays; the others were down dark hallways with neither electricity nor heat. They could search twenty rooms today; the remaining eighty would have to wait until the sun was up tomorrow. That pushed their remaining time to the limit.

They split the rooms into two or three each, allowing them to finish within half an hour, plenty of time for them to gather as a family on Christmas evening. As they rose to leave the library, Benevolence said, "I pray you'll find what you're seeking."

"Thank you, Mother," Aidan replied, and as he went into the hall, he fell behind the others and stopped in his tracks.

"Wait, guys!" he called to them. "Wait here a minute." He ran back into the library.

"Mother, what did you say a moment ago?"

She smiled. "I said I pray you'll find…"

"You *pray*? I've never heard you use that phrase. You're not a religious person. Are you telling me something?"

She smiled. "They're simply words, my child."

"Are you pointing us back to the church? Are you giving me a clue?"

She turned away and gazed into the fire until Aidan gave up and left.

He told the others, and Noelle said she'd call the church before dinner and arrange for a key so they could go at daybreak. For now, they fanned out through the hallways, going to their assigned rooms to search.

Fifteen minutes later there were shouts from somewhere upstairs that resounded down the ancient halls. Everyone ran to the source of the noise and found Aidan standing in the hallway outside the bedrooms.

"I found it! I found the plaque!" He pointed to an open doorway just down the hall from Nicholas's bedroom.

"The chapel!" Tiona said. "That was Mother's clue! That was what the word 'pray' was about!"

They filed into the room, its walls lined with heavy tapestries that created a claustrophobic closeness and muffled their voices. Aidan pointed to the side wall of an altar at one end, where a dark piece of marble hung, obscured by gauzy curtains. He moved closer, raised his flashlight and read.

THE LAST CHRISTMAS

This marble pedestal is erected the ninth day of November in the year of our Lord Seventeen Hundred Forty-Six. It is dedicated to Prince Charles Edward Stuart and the brave men who fought and died in battle at Culloden. May this monument one day contribute to the cause and allow the crowning of the rightful monarch of Scotland. To God be the glory in every thing. Dedicated by Malcolm, chief of Clan Dayne.

Steph didn't understand, Jill said it made no sense, and Noelle agreed at first, but said it was obviously important and they should discuss every single word of it. After Aidan shot a picture, they returned to the great room, where the drink trolley awaited them.

Malcolm stood near the windows with a smile on his face, listening as Aidan read each word aloud and they searched for hidden meanings. The first sentence needed no explanation, and the second — the dedication — was to Bonnie Prince Charlie and the Jacobites. The line after that was the enigmatic one.

May this monument one day contribute to the cause and allow the crowning of the rightful monarch of Scotland.

Nicholas turned to Malcolm and said, "We've found the plaque. If we figure out the meaning, can you tell us?"

"I am forbidden," the old fellow reminded him. "But Benevolence has no such constraints."

They broke that sentence down word for word. How would a monument "contribute" and "allow the crowning"? Those were the perplexing questions, answers to which might solve the puzzle. Each felt a buzz of excitement to think they might be getting close.

"Let's talk about the date," Noelle suggested. "November 1746. The Jacobite defeat at Culloden was in April. Prince Charles went on the run, the gold arrived from France soon thereafter, and it went from one clan chief to another. What if the Dayne clan took control of it in the fall of 1746, around the same time as the base of the statue was built?"

Nicholas jumped up, catching his drink just as it was about to topple. "That's it! That's it, isn't it, Benevolence? The base has something to do with the gold." He looked at the others. "Anyone remember what it's made of? Maybe it's pure gold!"

"That's not the answer," Tiona recalled. "It's some kind of dark stone, maybe marble or granite."

"Maybe the marble hides a solid gold base." He paused, snapped his fingers and said, "I've got it! The gold is hidden *inside* the base. Malcolm was clan chief, and when he received the gold, he built a base for Mary's statue. It housed the gold, and all these years it has been hidden in plain sight in the village square. Am I right, Benevolence?"

They all turned to Benevolence, whose face was impassive. In a moment she put her hands together and began to clap. It was the only sound in the room until everyone started cheering.

CHAPTER TWENTY-NINE

"Excellent work, everyone," Malcolm said, taking center stage in front of the fireplace so he could address the family. "There is much I can reveal to you now, within the confines of my agreement not to aid and abet your efforts.

"The French gold came from Charles Stuart's brother, Henry, who was living in France and funding the rebellion as best he could. The stories about it being passed from family to family are true — the MacPherson clan chief brought it to me for safekeeping. There were several bags, each containing gold Louis d'or coins. Knowing that English troops were in the area and could come knocking at any moment, hiding it in the castle was a risky venture. The more people who learned of its existence, the more chance there was of word getting out or someone getting killed. That much gold can change a man from friend to foe.

"There was a centuries-old cairn near Torcall Castle that was the perfect place to hide the loot for a brief period. My brothers and I buried it, covered the hole with heavy stones, and it became our temporary hiding place."

At the time he took possession, Malcolm had no way to know how long it would be his to guard. He was to protect it until it was needed, perhaps for a second rebellion, or the glorious return of Charles Stuart to Scotland, or the mounting of an army for another battle like Culloden, this one with a better outcome.

"My brothers and I already planned to add a base to Queen Mary's statue, and we thought of a perfect plan. We made slight changes to the construction, instructing the masons to make a hollow place in the middle. They thought it was to save on costs, but the waterproof core became a secret vault.

"The workmen took the base into the village, and that night we dug up the gold and carted it to town. The base sat in the square where Mary's statue would be lifted atop it the next morning. We pried up the heavy marble slab that formed the base's lid and packed the bags snugly inside. With the top in place, no one knew what lay underneath. The next day our laborers used ropes to raise the queen to her new perch, her feet standing atop a fortune in gold. Gold that she guards to this day."

He chuckled at the thought. "We were clever, there's no denying it. Months passed with occasional skirmishes as Redcoats marched through the Highlands, but with Bonnie Prince Charlie off in France, they no longer vandalized property or searched our homes. Their visits were more to remind us we were under English rule and had better behave ourselves. Only once did they ask about a hoard of gold. They had heard the story and were half-heartedly looking for it. When an officer insisted on searching the castle to look for gold, I taunted him, saying he was in the wrong country. Ireland is where you'll find pots of gold. They're at the end of a rainbow, I told him, and he huffed away without further incident.

"As the years went by, clan chiefs died, new ones arose, and over time the rumor of a cache of gold became a folk legend. I died too, but thanks to my pact with Clootie — the devil, as you'll recall — I remained here to protect the castle. From then until now, the gold has been secure."

Nicholas asked why revealing it was important now.

"Because time is running out. The castle needs tending to. There must be household staff and workers for the pastures. If the earl — yourself, milord — is going to live here, he must have resources. Prince Charlie is long gone. So, it appears, are hopes for Scottish independence. The gold is long forgotten, and there is nothing to stop our clan from making use of it."

"I'm not living here…" Nicholas began, but Malcolm held up a hand.

"I'll hear no more of such talk for now," the old clan chief said dismissively.

Jill asked him if a Louis d'or was some kind of gold. She'd never heard the term.

The old man's eyes shone with excitement. "Years pass and things change, but the gleam of gold will never dim. Excuse me a moment." He walked out of the room and returned with an old, bulky book that looked like a Bible. He put it on a table and said, "This book has sat on a shelf in the library for centuries. Who can read French?"

Steph and Jill raised their hands, and Poppy rolled her eyes. Of course the rich bitches could read French.

"Come look at the title," Malcolm teased. "Tell everyone what it says."

"*A Complete History of Medieval France,*" Steph translated. "Sounds boring."

"It does indeed." Malcolm laughed. "That's why we chose it. No one has plucked this book from the shelf since I put it there in 1749. Do the honors, young lady. Open it."

She opened the cover and turned a few of the pages until she came to a surprise. The middle was hollow — someone had cut a large hole in it. Inside lay a rotting piece of cloth that had once been a bag, and a handful of coins that once had been its contents.

"Those are Louis d'or gold coins," Malcolm said. "You may pass them among yourselves. When we hid the gold, my brothers and I removed these few as a precaution. If times were hard, or payoffs must be made, we had a few coins from the cache to use ourselves. With so many bags and so many coins, no one would have noticed their disappearance."

"They're beautiful," Tiona said, turning a shiny coin over and over. "1740, can you imagine? This coin is almost three hundred years old and it looks brand new."

"That's the beauty of gold," Nicholas commented. "It never rusts or tarnishes." To Malcolm he said, "How much does each coin weigh?"

The man gave him a number in a medieval weight system, which Nicholas converted by searching the web. "Twenty-two hundredths of an ounce," he said. "Four and a half coins would equal an ounce of gold."

Poppy asked Malcolm what the coins were worth, but he had no way of knowing. The value of gold today was far different from the mid-seventeen hundreds. Purchasing power, inflation, fluctuation in value — those terms were Greek to a long-dead Scottish soldier.

Nicholas counted the coins hidden in the book. There were forty-two, and he calculated the weight in ounces, multiplied it by the recent price of gold — something important to know in his line of work — and took a deep breath.

"Do you know how many coins there are in the base?" he asked Malcolm, who answered that they had attempted to count one bag. He and his brothers had poured out the coins, counted until they grew weary, and replaced the gold. Their total was almost a thousand Louis d'or coins, which represented perhaps half of what one bag held.

"Okay, let's use two thousand as the number. How many bags were there?"

"Forty-five."

There was a collective gasp throughout the room. Malcolm and Benevolence smiled at their surprise.

"Forty-five bags?" Nicholas stammered, pecking at his calculator. "Let's see. Forty-five bags, two thousand coins in a bag, four and a half coins equal an ounce of gold, two thousand dollars an ounce at today's prices…" He pressed a button.

"Oh my God." He stumbled as his knees gave way, and he fell into a nearby chair and recalculated the numbers another time.

"How much is it?" Noelle cried. "Tell us!"

"Each bag has thirty pounds of gold. Pounds, not ounces. At two thousand dollars an ounce, thirty pounds is worth around a million US dollars."

Steph shouted, "There's a million dollars in that statue in town? Are you shitting me?"

"Hold it, honey," Nicholas said. "You're not even close."

"I knew it," Poppy smirked. "There's a catch to it."

Nicholas took a deep breath. "You're absolutely right, Poppy. There's a catch to it. *Each bag* holds thirty pounds of gold worth a million dollars. The total is around forty-five million dollars."

That statement shocked them all.

Tiona was the first to speak. "How is this possible? Mother, you told us there was a million pounds we had to find. How could you have been so far off?"

"I'm no businesswoman," Benevolence replied with a smile. "What I said was that it was a million, perhaps more. It seems I underestimated the total a bit. Now it's getting quite late. I'm off to bed."

CHAPTER THIRTY

Malcolm took his leave soon after Benevolence. The adults refreshed their drinks — most making doubles this time, given the revelations — and Noelle asked Nicholas what it all meant.

"You're laird of the castle," she said to her brother. "We agreed to split what we thought was a million quid. Aidan didn't show up in time, so it was to be the three of us…"

"Wait a minute!" Aidan's girlfriend screamed. "You can't cut us out of this like that!"

"*Us?*" Aidan said to Izzy. "We've known each other a month. We can discuss this later between ourselves, but you have no say in this discussion. I owe you for the plane tickets. That's it."

"And without me, you wouldn't be here at all. I deserve —"

"You deserve reimbursement, and that's what you'll get. I agree the plane tickets were important, but neither of us could imagine what happened. This is a family matter. If you want to stay, then shut up. If you can't do that, go upstairs."

Pouting, Izzy crossed her arms and sat back in her chair.

"Apologies, everyone," he said. "Noelle, please go on."

"All I was saying is, there's so much money now. What do we do from here?"

Nicholas gathered his thoughts. "As leader of the family, the decisions fall on my shoulders. I'll offer ideas, I'll consider the input of my siblings, and I hope we can unanimously agree how to deal with this unbelievable turn of events.

"The first consideration is whether to remove the gold. Given that the base of a statue in a tiny village on our estate contains more than forty million dollars in gold coins, the risk of leaving it in place seems too great to me. There's the family aspect — our ancestor Malcolm put it there for the Jacobite cause — but now that's ancient history. Whatever becomes of the gold, we should move it to a safe place. Does anyone disagree?"

No one did.

"Next comes disposition of the cache. I assigned a value to the Louis d'or coins using the base price of gold, which is around two thousand dollars an ounce. Prices go up and down, and we could face a potential loss of value should gold take a fall. And there's another critical component: the numismatic value. The coins are very old. Perhaps they're rare — a coin dealer can tell us that. It's possible that coins from the seventeen hundreds are worth far more than their weight in gold."

He paused for questions and continued. "I propose we immediately remove the coins to a major bank, perhaps in Glasgow or Edinburgh, and that I hire a rare coin dealer to appraise them."

Noelle asked about taking the hoard to London or New York, where it might be easier for an expert to value them, but Nicholas thought there could be enormous hurdles in trying to remove that much dollar value in coins from Scottish soil. They would be required to declare them, and regardless, the government was sure to get involved once word got out.

"There's no assurance they'll award us custody of the gold," he said. "There are laws governing the discovery of national treasure, and the government may fight for the lion's share of the cache. We have tax implications to consider. We could never remove this much treasure from the country without governmental approval. If we did otherwise, I guarantee we'd end up in prison. We will need advice from our attorneys and accountants as soon as we uncover the hoard."

Nicholas glanced at his watch. Almost midnight. Time had flown on this monumental Christmas evening, one they would never forget.

"Since tomorrow's our last day here, I must line up several things," he said. "I'm going to bed and get started first thing in the morning. There's one last thing I'd like us to settle tonight. Are we going to split the proceeds three ways as we agreed because Aidan did not arrive on time, or four? I'll give you my thought, but I'd like to hear yours first. Aidan, you may speak last. Noelle, please begin."

"I need the money. I'm living hand to mouth despite owning a popular restaurant. Earlier we were splitting a million, but now things are different. Now it's forty-five, for God's sake. Plenty for everyone and then some. Unless the government takes it all, we're rich. I say give Aidan a share."

Tiona was next, and she brushed a tear away. "I'm poorer than you, sis. Before tonight, I was mentally calculating my third of a million pounds. Perhaps four hundred thousand dollars before taxes, right? Then the IRS takes maybe a third, leaving me two something. That wasn't enough to improve my life by much. All it might mean was a little better apartment, nicer clothes and eating in actual restaurants instead of ordering Chinese takeout.

"Now look where we are. Should Aidan get a fourth of the loot? Why the hell not? He helped us, and like Noelle said, we're all rich. So I get ten million before taxes, six or seven afterwards? Or the government takes half and I'm left with three million net. Bring it on, baby. I'm set."

Nicholas said, "You're next, Aidan, and you already have two votes in favor. Anything to add?"

"Yours is the final say, Nicky. What I think doesn't matter. How do you vote?"

"We all contributed to the hunt, so we each get a share. That's my decision. Now it's off to bed."

Izzy let out a war whoop, realized how inappropriate her action was, and grinned like a Cheshire cat.

CHAPTER THIRTY-ONE

Boxing Day — December 26

With no set time for breakfast having been announced, the family members arrived in the dining room in stages. Aidan was first, sitting at the table with coffee, toast and jam when Carly joined him around seven thirty.

"How long have you been down?"

"All night, to tell the truth. I slept on the couch in the library. Isabella went bonkers on me last night. We had an argument, and I left."

"I'm sorry, Aidan. Was it about the money?"

"What else? Tiona and Noelle claim to be poor, but they don't know what poor is. I left home at sixteen without graduating or a plan. I wanted to be on my own, out from under Mother's thumb, and as far from the castle as I could get. I blew most of my savings on a one-way ticket and ended up in rural New Mexico.

"Twenty-three years later, I've very little to show for myself, at least by your standards. I live in the boondocks in a rented trailer, deal cards in a casino, and drive a 1986 pickup. But I'm free, I see snowcapped mountains from my porch every morning, and I answer to nobody. I've had women in my life, but it's never been serious. I like Izzy, but she's twenty-four and I'm nearing forty. We met in a bar a month ago. I hardly know her, and allowing her to come was a mistake. Then again, she's the reason I got to be here. So it could be that I owe her everything. That's her logic, anyway."

Carly disagreed, saying none of them could know how Benevolence's invitation would turn out. "Be noncommittal, get back home, and do whatever you decide is right by her. We all have decisions to make, and what you don't need is someone else making them for you."

Izzy came through the doorway in a ragged T-shirt and sweatpants. She flopped down in a chair beside Aidan and demanded, "Get a servant in here. I want coffee."

Nicholas walked in behind her. "Good morning, all. Did everyone sleep well?"

Izzy complained, "I couldn't sleep. TMI from last night, I guess. Nicky, when do we…I mean when does Aidan get his gold?"

"It's Nicholas," Carly snapped. "Only the family calls him Nicky."

"What-*ever*. How about an answer, *milord*?"

Nicholas said much work remained, and the gold was none of her affair. Whatever information Aidan shared was his business. She pouted and drank her coffee.

Within fifteen minutes the rest had arrived, and everyone was having breakfast. Benevolence joined them and cornered Nicholas, inquiring about his plans for the family's last day at Torcall Castle.

"With what's been revealed, you must stay on," she insisted. "The requirement that everyone leave by six tonight no longer applies to you. There are five days remaining to establish your residency and break the curse. For me and my faithful servants, the time expires tonight. Our one-year extension of life ends at sundown."

Nicholas looked at Carly, who gave him a nod, and he said, "I had intended to speak to all of you later today, but here we are. Benevolence has teased the elephant in the room, and therefore I'll deal with it now. Isabella, you are excused. You're not part of the family, and the matters before us are confidential."

She glared at him from across the table, jabbed Aidan, and said, "Honey, tell them I'll be part of the family soon enough. Make your brother let me stay. Take a stand for me."

"Go," Aidan muttered. "I'll catch up with you later."

She stormed out of the room past Barclay, who held the door and closed it behind her.

"Sorry about that," Aidan said. "Seems all I do is apologize…"

Tiona moved to the chair next to him, squeezed his arm and said, "Hey, bro. You can't blame her. She sees the gold ring, pardon my pun, and she's trying to grab it. Looks like you have a decision to make about your friend."

Nicholas told them he'd gotten little sleep, with so much left to do in their one remaining day. "I was on the phone at six thirty this morning, making arrangements to move the gold," he explained. "At one o'clock we're meeting a crew from Inverness in the village square. It would have been easier to find workers in Mallaig, but I shied away from the local guys. Mallaig's too close to Torcall Castle. Inverness is a hundred miles from here, and I'm hoping that extra distance will limit the rumor mill.

"I expected it would be difficult getting people to work on a holiday, but doubling their normal rate did the trick. Nothing much excites me anymore, but I am anxious to see what's inside that base."

He continued. "All of you will leave for Glasgow tonight by six. My family and Tiona will fly to Heathrow and spend the night in a hotel. Aidan, you told me you and Izzy are flying direct to the states from Glasgow. I'm staying on…"

Benevolence beamed. "I was certain you'd do it."

"You're wrong. I *won't* do it. I'm staying a few more days to be sure everything's worked out with the gold. This morning I'll arrange a secure facility in Glasgow to store it. God willing, it'll be there tonight. As soon as possible I'll meet with our advisors and head home on the twenty-ninth."

Benevolence said, "What about the curse? You're dooming your own family."

"Malcolm's pact with the devil? If there really is a curse, and this is not simply a ruse to lure me back, it happened in the seventeen hundreds. Things were different. How far away from home did people venture? A hundred miles? Two hundred? If a clan chief wasn't living in the castle, chances are he resided somewhere nearby. Mallaig, or perhaps Inverness. A trip home to Torcall Castle required less than a day's ride on horseback.

"The curse has vastly different implications in the twenty-first century. In the first place, nobody believes in curses these days. Or wizards who cast spells. Or the doom of a clan and its ancestral home simply because a New York executive won't stop his life and come live in seclusion in this Godforsaken part of rural Scotland.

"If the curse exists, which I doubt, it doesn't apply to me. If that premise is incorrect, I accept the responsibility. Times have changed, Benevolence. Vast changes occurred in the sixty-something years since you and I were born, and unbelievable ones in the three hundred years since Uncle Malcolm's lived. That's why I will pledge to act as leader of the family — 'clan chief,' if you want to use that antiquated term — and help with decisions about the future both of the gold and this castle. But I refuse to live here, whatever the consequences."

"It's a selfish decision," she muttered as she handed a thick envelope to each of them. "Here's the twenty thousand pounds I promised you on Boxing Day. It's my bequest to my children and stepchildren. Perhaps there will be far more soon, but if you are disappointed when you open the base, at least you received something on the last Christmas.

CHAPTER THIRTY-TWO

Morning clouds gave way to sunshine, and by afternoon the weather was perfect for the task at hand. Nicholas and his siblings plus Carly, Izzy and the girls stood in the village square. Six workers from Inverness stood near a pickup and the light crane they'd brought. Two miles up the hill at Torcall Castle, far enough away to avoid spectators, sat an armored truck from Glasgow. In the square near Nicholas stood two tall, swarthy men who wore long black trench coats. These men came from Glasgow too — they worked for a private security service that provided armed guards for sensitive projects.

In most municipalities, moving a statue in the square would require permits and town council approval. Not so at Torcall. As the earl, Nicholas Dayne's orders superseded everything else. The mystified villages watched the crane back into place and men affix cables to Mary's effigy. An old woman cried, "Why are you taking her down?" and Nicholas stepped before the people.

"There are structural issues in the base," he lied. "Our monarch is leaving her post but not abandoning it. I promise you she will be back in her usual place by teatime."

Once the statue had been removed, the workers brought the pickup truck in close and erected a seven-foot fence covered with plastic sheeting around their work area. Nicholas told the villagers it gave the workmen space to do their jobs. That feeble explanation was all he could come up with, and the doubting townspeople whispered among themselves, asking why the earl had invaded their peaceful village on the day after Christmas.

Nicholas, his family and the guards waited inside the enclosure and Tiona took pictures. The burly workmen took crowbars to the marble slab on top, pried it up, gathered around all sides, and removed it with a mighty heave. Nicholas had warned the family to remain impassive no matter what they saw. As Malcolm had said, the middle of the base was hollow and stuffed with bags made from heavy burlap that had remained intact for centuries, protected from moisture and the elements.

Nicholas worried that the ancient bags might disintegrate when moved, which was the main reason for erecting the privacy fence. Although the people couldn't see, the six men removing the gold might get a glimpse of gold, but the two guards with semiautomatic rifles under their coats would ensure everything went smoothly.

Nicholas had calculated the weight of each bag at around thirty pounds, depending on how many coins it contained. He moved in and instructed two workers to lift the top bag out carefully. He held his breath as one cradled it and passed it to a second, who laid it gingerly in the pickup's bed.

"One down, forty-four to go," Tiona quipped as the men lifted the second bag, then the third and fourth. By the time twenty lay in the truck, the men had to use a stepstool to reach inside and access the sacks at the bottom.

Things proceeded without issue until the removal of the thirty-eighth bag. Unbeknownst to anyone, it had been torn when being placed in the base in 1746. When one of the men picked it up, the bag collapsed and a shower of gold coins cascaded onto the remaining sacks. They found every nook and cranny, disappearing deep into spaces between the bags.

"Oh my God," Nicholas cried as he summoned the two security guards. "Just when things were going so well."

The laborers were shocked. One reached down and scooped up a handful of Louis d'ors. "Look at this! Somebody hid these in here? Are the bags full of coins? What are they?" He showed them to the other men, leaving Nicholas scrambling for an answer that wouldn't make things worse.

"Put them down!" he shouted. "They're ancient..."

"Pirate gold, that's what I say!" a workman declared. "We uncovered treasure!"

Now realizing their purpose for being here, the guards moved their hands to the weapons inside their coats as Nicholas pulled the crew chief aside. "We must get this job finished quickly, and they have to keep quiet. Tell your men I'll double their pay if they keep this to themselves." He knew that last request was futile, but he had to buy a little time. Once the gold arrived at the Glasgow vault, everything would be fine.

Under the watchful eye of the guards, the men gathered up the loose coins, tossing Jacobite gold into a rusty bucket that someone retrieved from the bed of the pickup. They removed the remaining bags, and within the hour the work ended without further incidents. One had been sufficient for a lifetime, Nicholas commented as the family had nervously observed the men. Now forty-four bags and a bucket of gold lay in the pickup bed.

Nicholas climbed the small ladder, peered inside to ensure it was empty, and ordered the men to replace the marble top. Then the security guards assembled the workers who had handled the gold and ordered them to turn their pockets inside out.

"Is that necessary?" Nicholas asked, but withdrew his objection when three gleaming coins fell to the ground.

"You've just lost your job," the foreman growled to the culprit, but Nicholas stopped him, saying he didn't blame the man.

"I'm going to give each of you a thousand quid as a bonus," he said. "It more than doubles your pay for this job, and it's meant to buy your silence. These coins date back to the time of Bonnie Prince Charlie, and they're priceless pieces of Scottish history. Some may eventually be displayed in the national museum in Edinburgh. Thank you for your work today, and I ask you not to discuss this with anyone."

The men appreciated the gesture, although it would not accomplish Nicholas's aim. They were already whispering among themselves. They had witnessed something few men would ever see — a real, honest-to-goodness treasure cache. Back in Inverness tonight, there was no doubt all their friends would hear about this day.

CHAPTER THIRTY-THREE

The foreman had been told what came next. The two guards commandeered the pickup filled with gold, pulled a tarp over the treasure, backed the truck out of the enclosure, and drove away, with the family following in the Rolls. At the castle, the guards and the men in the armored truck transferred the intact bags. Nicholas watched the move, tallying each bag on a slip of paper. When they finished, he carried the metal bucket filled with coins inside.

Down in the village, the crew dismantled the privacy fence and raised the statue up onto its base. Everything was back in place, the only difference being that the base had forty-something million dollars less gold inside than before.

With the Dayne family now absent, the villagers approached the workers and asked what they did behind the fence. Some might have bragged except for the supervisor's stern glare. "We just repaired the base," they said as they finished their work, swept up around the statue, and waited for their truck to return. An hour later, Nicholas returned the truck to the square, and the workers left for Inverness.

The armored vehicle left Torcall Castle for Glasgow, and four hours later it rolled down an incline into a sub-basement of the National Bank of Scotland. Guards with automatic rifles surrounded the truck as the bags were transferred to a cart, then taken into a secure vault. The shipment was safe, a bank officer reported to Nicholas by telephone.

By four p.m. on Boxing Day, the town square was empty. The villagers were in their homes or one of Torcall's two pubs, gossiping and speculating about what they surmised happened behind the fence. There had been the occasional shout, and someone yelled the words "pirate treasure." That had gotten the crowd's attention.

Not pirate booty, but the lost crown jewels of Scotland were hidden in the base of Queen Mary's statue all these years, some men said. The Dayne clan put it there, and now they were claiming the hoard for themselves.

Others wondered if the Sinclairs had hidden treasure here like at Rosslyn Chapel. Not treasure, someone else suggested. Something of far greater value — the Holy Grail, the cup touched by the lips of our dear Savior Himself. Everyone crossed themselves as exciting theories and rounds of drinks flowed until closing time.

The laborers — those who had seen treasure with their own eyes — were back home in Inverness, a hundred miles away from Torcall, bragging about the thousand-pound bonus they had been paid for their silence, a bargain they were powerless to keep. In half a dozen pubs scattered throughout the city, men regaled their mates with a story of forty-five bags packed to the brim with gold coins. Where was this fabulous treasure trove discovered? the people asked. It was a tiny village just down the road from Torcall Castle, the ancestral home of the Dayne clan. The town bore the same name as the castle.

Torcall Village was the place. Suddenly an obscure town was a place of mystery and possibility. If there was a fortune in gold hidden in a statue, or the Grail, or the crown jewels, then what other secrets could there be?

While the highlands were abuzz with speculation, it was a somber time at Torcall Castle. Boxing Day was drawing to a close, and that meant the family must honor Benevolence's requirement that they depart. Nicholas had received a reprieve, although he would not fulfill his obligation to live in the castle. In fact, he would arrive in New York on the twenty-eighth, just two days behind his wife and daughters. If the curse that protected the castle and the clan ended on December thirty-first, then so be it. He had his own life to live.

The gold created a number of things for Nicholas to deal with in his remaining time. He arranged a meeting for tomorrow afternoon with the family's solicitors and chartered accountants to consider the next steps. The advisors were unaware of the purpose of his quickly arranged meeting, and Nicholas wondered how they'd react when they learned about the cache.

The family gathered one last time in the great room, two hours before their departure time. Nicholas had assigned the three girls to count the gold coins in the bucket, and they sat on the floor, making piles and tallying numbers on a sheet. When they finished, they had counted two thousand three hundred forty-one coins. He'd been using two thousand as a round number in his earlier calculations, and now it appeared the cache might be even larger than they thought.

He did the calculations. The coins they counted weighed five hundred and twenty ounces and were worth just over a million dollars. That was one bag, and there were forty-four more. His earlier calculation was right on the money. Around forty-five million total.

By half past five, Barclay and John had the suitcases loaded in the car. There were tearful, heartfelt embraces between the family members who had been apart for a decade, and also kind words for Benevolence, the mother and stepmother whom they would never see again. They hugged Cook, Mrs. Campbell, and Barclay, the beloved servants of the Dayne children's childhoods, who would be leaving with the lady they had served for so many years.

Even the newcomers Laris and John were emotional. They had experienced a lifetime of unbelievable things in a few short days, and they genuinely hoped to see the family again. Nicholas had asked the couple to continue working at the castle for as long as it stood. Perhaps that would be five days — until the stroke of midnight on the last day of the year — but he hoped it might be for many years to come.

The staff and Nicholas stood in front of the castle and waved goodbye as the Rolls pulled away. As the car drew out of sight, Nicholas heard the clock pealing in the church tower of the village. It rang the hour, beat by beat. Six long peals echoed through the valley.

Six o'clock.

He turned to walk indoors with the others, but it was only him, Laris and John.

———

They sat in the great room. John added a log to the fire and stoked it a bit, then sat on the couch next to his wife, who had fetched the beverage trolley and fixed Nicholas a Scotch. Their discomfort at hobnobbing with the laird was evident, and Nicholas tried to assuage the situation.

"They're really gone," he mused as Laris and John awkwardly grasped their wineglasses. He'd insisted they join him for a drink, and although they were well accustomed to handling a pint of ale, sipping wine from dainty crystal glasses was uncomfortable. Laris whispered to John to be careful not to break anything, because the laird might take the cost from their wages.

She answered Nicholas. "Yes, Lord Dayne, it appears Lady Dayne's pronouncement was correct. It seems…" She paused. "It seems strange to have this huge old castle all to ourselves, although we've had a year to prepare for this night."

"I agree. It's a depressing change from having my family here, enjoying Christmas, trying to solve the clues my father wrote, and overseeing the exciting work in the village today. The past few days our minds have been reeling with activity. I rather prefer it that way, but here we are."

John apologized in advance if he was out of line, but asked what Nicholas planned to do next. "Will you stay on, milord? You enlisted us to remain here, but Laris and I are only two people in a huge old castle. We will need help."

"I'll arrange as much help as you need. You're young and eager, but also new at all this. I understand how you must have depended upon the others — Cook, Mrs. Campbell and Barclay — to guide you both. It might be best to bring in an older couple who've managed a large house before. You'd be equals in status, but their experience could be beneficial."

They agreed, and then Laris asked to be excused, saying she had to prepare his meal.

"With everyone gone, I seem to have lost my appetite," Nicholas replied. "Finish up here and go on home, both of you. It's been a long day. I'll see you in the morning."

They closed the door and left Nicholas staring into the flames. Regardless of his refusal to move into the castle permanently, he was still the head of the Dayne clan, and in his gut he didn't believe old Malcolm's tale about a curse. Was he doing the right thing?

It'll be ten years ago on New Year's Eve that my father died. After his funeral, I never returned. My life is in America, not in the remote highlands of Scotland. I love my work and my life. Carly and I can buy anything or go anywhere we want. I will not trade my life for this, nor would I ask my wife to do it.

He reached for the cigar and cutter beside him, lit up, and took a long, satisfying puff.

Someone spoke. "The reason why you have to live here is that it will all disappear without you."

Malcolm sat in an armchair over near the windows. How long he had been there, Nicholas couldn't say. The man had read his thoughts, but why should Nicholas find that unusual, given everything that had transpired in the past few days?

"Move over here by the fire, Uncle," Nicholas said. "I need your advice."

The old warrior took a chair across from Nicholas and warmed his hands by the fire, which Nicholas found amusing, considering he was a ghost.

"At least part of the legend is true," Nicholas said. "Benevolence and the others are gone, as she said they would be. Yet you remain. How long will I have the pleasure of your company?"

Malcolm reminded Nicholas of their conversation on his first night at the castle. "I will remain here for as long as the castle stands, protecting both it and the clan. If a clan chief lives at Torcall Castle by year-end, I will remain. If the castle and the clan fall, then my work here is done."

Laris knocked, opened the door, and said they were leaving for the evening. Twenty minutes later John called on the phone line that ran from the gatehouse.

"I'm so sorry to bother you, milord, but there are people from the BBC standing outside the gate. They want to talk about the gold you found in the village today."

Damn the hides of those workers! I knew I shouldn't trust them to keep quiet, and after the gold spilled out everywhere, who could blame them for telling everyone what they saw? But now the BBC's gotten hold of it. Damn! Damn! Damn!

"Tell them I'll issue a statement in the morning," he told John. "It's nighttime and I'm not coming to the gate."

Malcolm tented his fingers in front of his face. "They won't wait for you, Nicholas. If you don't speak with them, they'll report what the workers found, and your side of the story — whatever you decide to say — will remain unheard."

"Sage advice from a man born in the seventeen hundreds," Nicholas said with a grin. "How do you know what the BBC will do?"

"I'm a spirit, but I have eyes and ears. Benevolence had a television set in her suite. She showed me how it works and what it is used for. A useful invention, although oftentimes annoying beyond words."

Nicholas smiled. "I'm not going to the gatehouse tonight. To be honest, I don't have anything to give them except the truth, which is what they already know. How about this? Tomorrow I'll confirm the story, explain that a ghost told me about it, and that we followed clues written by my deceased father."

"I presume that's an attempt at humor," the old man said.

"Not a very good one, I'm afraid. On that note, I'll call it a night. I need to get some sleep," Nicholas said to his phantom ancestor, who quipped that sleeping was overrated. He hadn't done it in over two hundred years.

CHAPTER THIRTY-FOUR

December 27

After a night of more tossing and turning than slumber, Nicholas stopped resisting and climbed out of bed around seven. Every time he traveled, he didn't sleep well on the first night without Carly in his bed. When he added the burden of the clan's existence that was on his shoulders, he felt like a truck had hit him.

He plodded downstairs in his pajamas and robe and found Laris in the kitchen. Thankful she had the coffee pot brewing, he asked if the BBC people were still at the gate.

"They left after they learned you wouldn't be coming to talk with them," she said. "And they promised to be back this morning. I had the telly on before I came over. It's all over the news, I'm sorry to say."

His advisors were due at Torcall Castle at two. By then they'd have heard about the gold. He considered that a good thing; perhaps they'd already be devising strategies to handle the situation.

After his shower, he dressed and called John at the gatehouse. One of those trucks with a satellite dish on top had just pulled up, the handyman said. A few people stood by the gate, awaiting his arrival. Nicholas said he'd be right there.

He had no prepared statement, but he was no stranger to extemporaneous speaking. He walked through the gate and stood before outstretched hands with microphones. The family became aware that something might be hidden in the statue's base, he told the eager reporters. He hired a crew to remove the effigy and examine the base, inside of which they found several bags of French coins dating to the 1740s.

"Were there thousands of gold coins?" someone shouted.

"Who told you they were in the base?" yelled another.

"Is it the lost Jacobite gold?" screamed a third.

There were gold coins, he said. They hadn't counted the coins, nor could they say who placed the bags there or when, so it was impossible to speculate on what they represented. He'd learned of their existence by deciphering clues he found in an old family history book.

"It is a fortune though, correct, Lord Dayne?"

"The word 'fortune' means different things to one man than it does to another. I will say that there were many gold coins, the worth of which I have no idea at this time."

"Where are they now?"

"They are safely stored in a vault. That's all I'll say about that."

"What do you plan to do with them?"

"I can't answer that," he said truthfully. "I'll be enlisting the advice of professionals, and I'm sure the government will have advice to offer as well. Now if you'll excuse me, I have work to attend to."

They yelled more questions as he turned his back and walked away.

"Nicky!"

Irritated that someone had the audacity to address him by that nickname, he whirled around.

"Nicky, wait up!"

He looked down the lane and saw someone waving as he ran full speed toward the gatehouse.

He put his hand up to shield his eyes from the morning sun. Who was it? The person drew near and he realized it was his half-brother Aidan.

"What the hell are you doing back? You should be on a plane to the States by now," he said as the reporters shot footage of a man they didn't recognize.

"Long story. Let's get away from the vultures and I'll explain."

Aidan shivered; he'd walked from the village in the damp morning chill. Laris fixed Aidan some hot tea, and Nicholas built a fire in the great room. Once he had his tea and was wrapped in a warm blanket, Laris left them alone. Aidan took a sip and explained.

"We all got to Glasgow last night, and your family and Tiona took the puddle jumper to London. We all said our goodbyes, and Izzy and I stayed at a hotel near the airport."

He paused for another drink of tea, and Nicholas said, "This should be interesting."

"We got up early because our flight was at half past six. Izzy had been a first-class bitch all morning. She pouted when I wouldn't tell her what was going to happen to the gold, even though I don't know myself. She accused me of not loving her — which is the truth, of course. I don't love her. I barely know her, for God's sake. Anyway, we got on the plane, took our first-class seats, and she started in on me again. She raised her voice to the point the flight attendant asked her to quieten down.

"Something snapped, I guess. I'm not one to do rash things, but I got up, told Izzy I was going to the loo, walked to the front of the plane, told the flight attendant I was having a panic attack, and asked if I could step out onto the jet bridge for a moment. She said yes, but make it quick, because the plane was ready to depart. I walked off and kept on going. I entered the terminal, and as I walked down the hall, I saw our plane back away from the gate.

"I had to pass through arrivals, and I was detained for a bit in immigration, but they decided I had broken no laws. All I did was abandon my bitchy girlfriend on the plane. The officers got a laugh out of that, stamped my passport, and sent me on my way. I still have Izzy's credit card from the earlier part of our trip, so I bought a bus ticket to Mallaig and paid a kid twenty pounds to drive me to the village, and there you have it."

Unable to help himself, Nicholas laughed and laughed. He apologized, but Aidan brushed it off. It was pretty funny, he admitted, saying he hoped every passenger on the plane hadn't gotten an earful all the way to the States. Izzy had to be one pissed-off female.

"What do you do next?"

Aidan shrugged. "I did the only thing that seemed right. I came back home."

"Then I'm putting you to work. We must decide what to do with our discovery. The advisors come at two. Let's put our heads together and be prepared for them."

CHAPTER THIRTY-FIVE

A sedan pulled through the gates and up to the castle at two, and out stepped two men and two women, each dressed in black business attire. Nicholas had met them all, and he introduced the four to Aidan.

They gathered at one end of the dining table, and the advisors spread out papers and laptops and cellphones. They had heard the news — it would have been impossible not to, one said — and they had discussed ideas as they rode up from Glasgow.

When they learned facts the reporters didn't know — including the value of the cache — they were astonished. Around forty-five million dollars — thirty-four and a half million pounds sterling — in old French gold coins was mind-boggling. Even the typically funereal solicitors couldn't mask their astonishment.

Nicholas asked for comments, and one accountant said, "It's a historical treasure, perhaps even the lost Jacobite gold. You must notify the archaeology people in Edinburgh and perhaps the National Trust and the museums."

A solicitor said, "Given that it's all over the news, I'm surprised you haven't gotten a call already."

"Where's the gold at the moment, Lord Dayne?" asked the younger solicitor, a man in his twenties.

"It's secure."

"How can you be sure? My point in asking is that we must ensure its safety."

"Trust me, young man," Nicholas replied. "The gold is in a vault and it is secure. The fewer who know the location, the better, no offense meant."

They discussed taxes, whether they'd be allowed to sell the gold, who might claim ownership of it under the law, and a dozen other logistical issues.

Nicholas felt his phone vibrate, and he glanced at a text from Carly. "Just arrived at home. Customs was a breeze, just like always. Smiley face." A deep sense of relief swept over him. His risky, top-secret plan had worked. Only now could he relax and give his full attention to the issues at hand.

After the girls counted the coins yesterday, he had split them, giving Noelle her one-fourth share worth a quarter million US dollars. She would have no problem carrying the coins back to London, but his wife was carrying three times that much gold — seven hundred and fifty thousand dollars' worth.

It was illegal to enter the United States with over ten thousand dollars in unreported currency or coins, but the ever-adventurous Carly had agreed to be the mule, and those traveling with her — even her daughters — were unaware of what her bag contained. Her text proved she had cleared customs without incident just as she'd expected, and that was welcome news. When Nicholas returned to New York, he would divide the coins and send Aidan and Tiona their shares.

The older solicitor watched Nicholas read the text and breathe a sigh of relief. "Is everything all right, Lord Dayne?" he asked, and Nicholas said yes, things were just fine.

Millions of dollars in gold remained to be dealt with, but at least the four Dayne children would get two hundred and fifty thousand dollars each in tax-free gold coins. Nicholas would instruct them how to sell the gold in small quantities to several coin dealers and avoid suspicion. A transaction over ten thousand dollars required ID, a social security number, and advising the IRS, so they'd keep things low-key. At least the ones who needed it most — Tiona, Aidan and Noelle — would have funds to stay afloat while he and the authorities sorted out the many millions that remained.

The accountant was droning on about tax consequences when Nicholas tuned back into the conversation. The tax authorities would surely be in touch soon, she said, and they'd invite Nicholas to come see them. "You won't have a choice in the matter, and I'd suggest you try to meet in Glasgow, where our firm and your solicitors can be by your side."

It was almost five when the advisors departed, and once Nicholas had escorted them out the door, Laris handed him a wad of notes. "You've had several calls," she advised. "This one on top has been rather insistent. He's called three times and became irritated when I wouldn't interrupt your meeting."

He called the Edinburgh number and heard the one-word answer. "Harkins."

"This is Nicholas Dayne, returning your call."

"Ah yes, Lord Dayne. Thank you for responding. Let me introduce myself, sir. I'm Cecil Harkins, head of tax for Revenue Scotland. I'll be in charge of your case…"

"My case? I wasn't aware I had a case."

The man chuckled. "Oh my, yes, presuming the BBC's got the story right. Did you unearth millions of pounds in gold on your estate yesterday?"

"Forgive me, Mr. Harkins. I returned this call to a number that might belong to anyone. Until I verify who you are and where you work, I'll be saying nothing. If you're who you say, stay by your desk. I'll call you back."

He disconnected, told Aidan what was going on, googled the main number for Revenue Scotland, called it, and asked to speak to Cecil Harkins. His call went to a secretary, and in moments the tax man was back on the line. Nicholas put the call on speaker for Aidan's benefit.

As the accountant had predicted, Harkins suggested a meeting at the head office in Edinburgh. He offered a date two days out, and Nicholas said he wouldn't be available, as he was returning to the States tomorrow.

"What other family member may we meet with?"

"None. We all live outside Scotland, as I'm certain you're aware. I can arrange for the family's accountant and solicitor to meet in Glasgow. If it fits my schedule, I'll join by Zoom."

The man's tone turned hard. "With all respect, milord, this is not about your schedule. You're in the midst of something quite important, as I'm sure you're aware. You may not leave the United Kingdom until we have our meeting."

Nicholas snapped, "I may not leave? Under what authority do you presume to detain me? As a British citizen, unless I'm under arrest, I'll damn well do whatever I choose."

Harkins backed off. "My apologies, Lord Dayne. I'm not suggesting you'd be detained, sir. I chose my words unwisely. It would behoove you to state your case before Revenue Scotland in person rather than to face seizure of your treasure trove pending a hearing. Perhaps that makes our position clearer."

"You have no idea where the gold is."

"Give us some credit, Lord Dayne. This is a first-world country, not a tax haven on some Caribbean island. Of course we know where it is. Yesterday you moved your cache to a vault at the National Bank of Scotland in Glasgow. I'm hoping for an amicable resolution between ourselves, sir."

Nicholas wanted to confer with his advisors and said he'd call Harkins back in the morning. He hadn't yet booked his return flight, and if he did so now, he wondered if he'd be allowed to leave. Was his passport already flagged for detention? Surely that couldn't happen without a judge's order, but there was no reason to cause friction. Since dealing with the taxing authorities was inevitable, cooperation was the best way to keep most of the gold for the family.

Aidan asked what he intended to do. "They could tie things up and keep us from getting anything for years, right?" he asked, and Nicholas said that was possible. He revealed that Carly had carried gold back to the USA, a third of which belonged to Aidan. At least they could enjoy a little of the money, as long as they were low-key and careful about how they converted and used it.

Malcolm emerged from somewhere across the room and took a chair between them. "You've truly decided not to stay?" he asked. "I'm disappointed in you."

"I can't do it, Uncle. I wish I felt differently about the importance of this matter. It's unfortunate, but the title of clan chief meant a great deal more back in your day than it does in mine. I'm the last of the earls. I have no male heirs, and I'm almost seventy. If I moved back home, all I'd be doing is prolonging the inevitable. When I'm dead, the clan dies along with me."

"Give it up." Aidan's words were almost a whisper.

"What?"

"Give up your title as Earl of Torcall. Abdicate your position as clan chief. If you don't want to do it, let it go."

Nicholas asked, "What good does that do?"

"If you abdicate, the title passes to me as your brother and the only other male. I'm right, aren't I, Malcolm?"

The old warrior smiled. "You are."

Nicholas didn't understand. "What are you saying? You want to move back here and live in the castle? You'll be the one who breaks the curse?"

"Sure. Why not? Being lord of the manor beats dealing cards at a casino."

CHAPTER THIRTY-SIX

The family advisors were still in the sedan on the way to Glasgow when Nicholas called the elder solicitor. He explained what they were considering, and the man promised to discuss it with the others and be in touch tomorrow morning.

Aidan asked if Nicholas had regrets about giving up his birthright, and he shook his head. He had a life and a career in New York, and he would have suggested it himself had there been an inkling Aidan was interested.

Nicholas said, "It never entered my mind. To be honest, you were in your sleeping bag on the doorstep with Isabella that first night. You've always been…no offense, Aidan, but you haven't struck me as being particularly motivated. We're opposites, and I don't mean to judge you. You're a free spirit, ready to let life lead you in whatever direction, and you are content with that. I'm driven by money and power and scoring the next big deal on Wall Street. Neither of us is right or wrong; we're just wired differently. I couldn't live your life, and I'll wager you couldn't live mine."

Aidan nodded. "Everything you've said is correct, and yes, you're right that I'm unmotivated. I'm accustomed to going with the flow, dealing with things — or choosing to ignore them — as they come at me. If I take this job, I'll need your help. There are lawyers and accountants, but when there's a crucial decision, I'll want my successful brother's input.

"You haven't been here since Father's death, and that tells me your direct involvement as the laird has been minimal. That means there are procedures in place that keep things running smoothly. I'm no manager, but I think I can oversee qualified people. Best of all, I can enjoy life in the peace and quiet of my childhood home here in remote Scotland. All I want out of life is contentment, and on that first morning when I walked into the village, I realized I might find it if I just came back home."

He continued, "I'm thirty years younger than you, and I hope to marry and have a family someday. Not Izzy, for God's sake. I want someone nice and easygoing who loves me instead of money. Maybe there'll be kids. A son, even, to carry on the family name and become earl himself. That's not inconceivable."

Given the complexities of dealing with a fortune in gold, Aidan said Nicholas must handle matters involving the treasure. That made sense to Nicholas too, and he said he'd postpone his departure for New York another day or two, allowing him time to meet with the tax man and the advisors.

Nicholas called Carly, explained how Aidan had dumped Izzy on the plane, returned to the castle, and the decision about his birthright. Aidan's decision surprised her, but she considered it a perfect solution.

With only three family members and two servants remaining in the drafty castle, the halls and rooms were eerily quiet. The Dayne men — two living and one dead — sat around the fire with cocktails in hand as Laris and John prepared dinner. They talked logistics, and Aidan broached a subject that worried him.

"You said my quarter share of the coins was safely in New York with Carly. That was a wonderful thing to do for us, but I doubt I'll go back for months. I can get someone in New Mexico to clean out the trailer and store what few things I own, but where will the money come from to run the castle?"

Nicholas said, "From the estate, as it always has. The accountants collect the rents and pay the staff and the bills. There's sufficient income to offset normal expenses, and if a catastrophe occurs, I'll be around to help you work it out. As far as your share of the gold, I've already thought of a plan for it.

"Upon my return, I'll set up a corporation that will establish a brokerage account at my firm. We'll mask the corporation's ownership, but it'll ultimately funnel back to you. The corporation will transfer a quarter million dollars — your share — into the brokerage account, and I'll make trades for you. Stocks, bonds, ETFs, the gamut, all open and aboveboard. We'll win some and lose some, but over the years I've done very well picking investments. I'll ensure the corporation pays its taxes on the profits, and you'll end up with a retirement account for yourself and a legacy for the future earl of Torcall, yet to be born!"

He said, "Well and good, but short-term cash is an issue. As I said, I used Izzy's credit card to get back here because I have no money. The twenty I paid the kid to drive me to Torcall was the last bill in my pocket."

"Do you have a bank account in New Mexico?"

"Yes, but I don't trust banks. I opened it so the casino could direct deposit my salary. I access the money through my debit card, but my last deposit was gone the minute it hit the account. As you can tell, I don't make a lot."

"No problem. Excuse me for a moment." Nicholas went upstairs and returned with his laptop. He got the account information from Aidan, entered everything into a banking program, and in a matter of minutes he said, "There. I put ten grand in your account. I suggest you go to Mallaig in a day or two and open a personal bank account denominated in pounds, not dollars. You're going to be living here, and it'll be the way I get cash to you for your own needs. Don't worry about trusting banks. They're avaricious bastards, but they won't make off with your money."

Aidan thanked him, and Nicholas assured his brother he'd put more in if Aidan needed it. "I'll pay you back once we settle the gold," Aidan said, but Nicholas shrugged it off, saying it was a small price to pay for Aidan's agreeing to change his entire life for the clan's sake.

Malcolm smiled as he listened to the half-brothers work things out. He didn't understand terms like credit cards, direct deposits, accessing money and salaries. But he got the gist of it. A catastrophe averted, the clan should face a rosy future.

CHAPTER THIRTY-SEVEN

December 29

The tax man Cecil Harkins balked at meeting in Glasgow but agreed once Nicholas explained he wanted his advisors present. At ten a.m., Aidan and Nicholas entered the Inland Revenue offices on Kilbride Street and were shown to a conference room. The solicitors and accountants who came to Torcall Castle were already there, and in a moment two men entered. Harkins introduced himself and the other fellow, an underling who would be the direct liaison with the family's advisors.

Three hours later, they had settled several matters. Nicholas was giving up his title in favor of his brother, and although he would continue to be the point person for the treasure trove, Harkins said Nicholas was free to return home so long as his brother stayed. Aidan had no plans to leave the country and promised to notify Harkins if he changed his mind.

Nicholas told the tax men his plans for the gold. He intended to remove a representative sample — perhaps two hundred of the estimated ninety thousand coins. He would hire a prominent coin dealer in Edinburgh to examine them and issue a report as to authenticity, value, and condition.

"The coins are part of Scottish heritage," Nicholas continued. "While they are in the numismatic dealer's hands, I'll ask someone from the National Museum to examine them. I can't imagine their wanting the entire cache, considering the security required to protect it in perpetuity, but if they're interested in some — and they promise to display them instead of storing them in a basement somewhere — I'd be amenable to that discussion."

Nicholas and Aidan signed a document promising the coins would remain in Scotland, and Harkins asked the family's advisors to present a proposal on how the hoard should be taxed. Nothing would be finalized until everyone agreed where the coins would end up, and that decision might be months or years away.

On the way back to Torcall Castle, Nicholas contacted British Airways and booked a flight tomorrow afternoon. In the morning John would drive him to Glasgow. He'd take a short flight to London and on to the USA, arriving in New York around five in the afternoon.

Carly called during cocktail hour to report that news outlets throughout the USA were covering New York financier Nicholas Dayne's discovery of a vast hoard of ancient Scottish gold. Reporters had flocked to their apartment building, and she had hired a private security firm to post guards in the lobby and outside their apartment. He said she'd done the right thing, and he'd deal with it when he returned tomorrow afternoon.

He also broke the news about how Aidan had dumped Izzy and returned to the castle.

The brothers spent the evening on matters involving their ancestral home and lands. Aidan took careful notes as Nicholas explained what things the solicitors handled versus the accountants, the timing and typical amount of rental income and expenses, and how to begin the search for an older couple to assist Laris and John in the day-to-day affairs of the castle. The young couple would move from the gatehouse into the main building in a few days, and Nicholas suggested Aidan consider opening Torcall Castle to tourists. As Benevolence had reminded him prior to Aidan's arrival, their father's will had prohibited tours for ten years after his death. But in two days those ten years would be over.

Nicholas envisioned refurbishing perhaps ten bedrooms for guests to rent, offering a full breakfast and a complimentary happy hour and nightly Scotch-tasting event in the great room. "The castle is remote," he continued, "but I think that will be a drawing card. They can walk along the cliffs and see the Isle of Skye in the distance. We should promote the village too — I promise you the pubs and shops would welcome the business. If guests want a nice dinner by the sea, Mallaig's only eight miles away. It has plenty of restaurants, and tourists can take the Jacobite steam train up and back to and from Fort William. It's a perfect way for visitors to arrive and leave, and John can meet them at the station in a vintage Rolls-Royce."

Aidan loved the idea, and Malcolm agreed it would be a popular destination, although he frowned upon commercializing the castle.

"You sound like Father." Nicholas laughed, and Malcolm huffed that it was clear he shared Geoffrey Dayne's views more than his offspring did.

The next morning the car stood in the driveway, his one suitcase loaded and the door open, as Nicholas, Aidan and Malcolm emerged from the castle. The half-brothers hugged, and Aidan said, "I hope you'll come visit."

Nicholas promised he would, saying it would be an easy trip from London, where he traveled often. "I'll be seeing more of Noelle too," he added, saying Aidan should try to do the same.

He turned to Malcolm and opened his arms, but the old warrior stepped back. "There'll be no hugging for this clansman," he snorted. "Affection is for the women. For me, it's enough to bid you Godspeed and a quick return."

Nicholas climbed into the Rolls, and as John drove away, he turned for a nostalgic look back at the castle. It was a beautiful old place, it was home, and he wished his brother every success.

CHAPTER THIRTY-EIGHT

December 30

Nicholas preferred the daytime flights back to the States. He never slept well on planes, and after every overnight flight to London, it took most of the next day before he felt refreshed. The return trips were a breeze — get settled in, read the newspapers, have lunch, watch a movie, read or work a little, and be in his Manhattan apartment by cocktail hour.

He always kept his phone turned off on the long-haul flights. He enjoyed first-class air travel, and he considered it a rare treat to have no calls, texts or emails to deal with. Anything needing attention could wait until he was on the ground.

The plane landed twenty minutes early, and Nicholas retrieved his rolling bag, thankful he'd sent the other luggage home with Carly and the girls. Having carry-on luggage meant avoiding a half-hour wait in baggage claim.

A BA representative with a cart met him at the gate and welcomed him home. He was through customs and immigration in twenty minutes, and he walked through sliding glass doors into the arrivals hall to the usual throng of family and well-wishers awaiting the passengers.

He saw his driver through the crowd, and when he turned in that direction, there came a shout, then another.

"Mr. Dayne, over here!"

"Nicholas Dayne! Can you comment on the allegations?"

What the hell was going on? He saw people rushing toward him — not one or two, but a dozen. Microphones in hand, video cameras on shoulders, TV station logos on jackets — everyone speaking at once and vying for his attention.

He'd seen the press mob celebrities before, right here in this arrivals hall, but it had never happened to him. What had he missed?

The NBC affiliate reached him first. "Mr. Dayne," the reporter shouted, "can you comment on the accusations against you?"

"What are you talking about? I just got off a plane."

"You don't know?" cried a second reporter. "You've been accused…"

A man in a black trench coat stepped in front of the reporter and flashed a shield. "Mr. Dayne, I'm Detective Giordino, NYPD. Please come with me, sir."

"Am I under arrest?"

"Not at the moment, sir. I'd just like to have a word with you. Please come with me and let's get away from this mob."

His driver approached, and Nicholas asked if he could hand over his suitcase. The cop said no and took the bag himself, telling the driver to hang tight for half an hour and they would be back.

"If I'm not under arrest, I respectfully decline to go with you. I don't know what's going on here. You can call my attorney."

"Have it your way, buddy," Giordino said, handing the suitcase back. "When things go south, don't forget I offered you the easy way." He turned and walked away as the eager newsmen made sure their cameras had captured everything.

The throng of reporters followed them to the parking garage and pushed against the windows of the limo as the driver sped away.

"What the hell was that about?" he asked as he turned on his cellphone. It dinged dozens of times, signaling missed calls, incoming texts and emails, and failed FaceTime calls.

The driver had no intention of getting involved. "Something about an assault, sir. That, and some missing gold. I didn't pay much attention."

The phone rang and Nicholas took Carly's call. He told her what had happened at the airport, and she said she'd tried a dozen times to reach him on the plane, but his phone was off. When they spoke last evening, she had mentioned the reporters at their building, but they wanted to talk about the gold. This was something different — something alarming.

"Nicky, you won't believe this. Isabella Watson — Aidan's Izzy — hired a criminal lawyer in Chicago. They held a news conference this morning, and she accused you of sexually assaulting her and holding her inside the castle against her will. Aidan too — you and he participated in the sex stuff."

The news stunned him. What a crock of lies. He'd thought Izzy was nuts before, but she had proven it.

"Don't come to the front of our building," she warned him. "There's a crowd on the sidewalk waiting for you. Somebody at BA leaked which flight you were on, and they'll pounce on you as soon as the car drives up."

Nicholas called his office. Same thing there, his assistant reported. They were in the lobby, but the security guards refused to allow them into the elevators, so the office was quiet.

He had the driver drop him three blocks from his apartment building and left the suitcase in the car with instructions to drop it at the office tomorrow. When he approached his building and saw the mob on the sidewalk,

Nicholas turned into a tiny park nestled between two skyscrapers, walked to the far end and entered an alley that led to his building's service entrance. He'd taken this route once in the past when reporters had hounded him for a story on one of his business deals.

He darted past a garbage truck idling in the driveway and through a pair of swinging doors. An empty hallway led past a ground-floor restaurant's kitchen and on to the service elevators. He entered the car and pressed the button for the twentieth floor.

When he reached their apartment, Carly handed him a martini, and he sat on the couch with his family. He asked how Izzy had acted after they left the castle. Carly said she and Aidan had been quiet on the car ride to Glasgow. They split off at the airport, as Carly, the girls and Noelle went to the British Airways counter and Izzy and Aidan to Icelandic for their overnight flight to Chicago.

Aidan had hugged everyone and promised to stay in touch, but Izzy had walked away without a farewell to any of them. "I figure she concocted her story on the flight home," Carly continued. "I can only imagine how pissed off she was after Aidan abandoned her.

She said Izzy apparently stayed in Chicago instead of going on to New Mexico. She hired a lawyer and had a morning press conference. Most of America had already learned the news about the rich New York financier who found a fortune in gold coins, and now she offered the icing on the cake.

"It appears the press found your story too tantalizing to resist. You're the top story on the evening news."

"And what are her allegations?"

"Aidan enticed her to come home with him for Christmas. She didn't realize 'home' was a castle, complete with a dungeon."

"Are you serious?"

"Wait," she said. "This is so ridiculous it would be funny if it didn't involve you. Turns out you live a double life. By day you're a New York investment banker. By night you're the lord of an ancient clan of Scottish warriors. Aidan is your dim-witted half-brother, who can't keep his schlong in his pants and does whatever you tell him. The innocent Isabella — poor child — never had a chance. Aidan lured her to the castle. You sex-starved maniacs locked her in the torture chamber and had your way with her."

"Nobody's going to believe that."

"That doesn't matter. It's for those people who read the *National Enquirer*, honey. They enjoy other people's misfortunes, even more so when they're the rich and famous. You're no Jeffrey Epstein, but at the moment the media wants to paint you that way because it's sensational."

"Where does the gold come into all this? Did I buy her silence with a bag of coins?"

"Quite the contrary. She was Aidan's common-law wife..."

He cried, "She was *what*? They've known each other less than a month!"

"Funny how the facts get omitted from a good yarn. Wait 'til you hear this one. After your family found the gold, you held a clandestine meeting in the old castle. You all discussed where to hide it and how to divvy it up. When she learned you planned to cut your halfwit brother, Aidan, out of his share, she spoke up. You got furious and threw her out, posting an armed guard at the door to keep her from hearing how she and her husband might get their rightful shares. All that after you had raped her in the basement. What a horrible lord you are, Nicholas Dayne!"

"God almighty, the woman's crazy."

"Oh yeah, but she's attracting a hell of a lot of attention. You know what she wants."

He nodded. "Money or revenge, and I'll bet it's the former. I'll call my lawyer in the morning..." His phone rang. "It's Aidan," he said as he put the call on speaker.

"Nicky. Jesus, Izzy's got me in a mess. I need your help!"

"I'm right there with you, in case you haven't heard the news."

"I have, and I'm so sorry she got you involved. A carload of cops from Mallaig came here this afternoon. They demanded to look around the castle."

"They can't do that without a warrant."

Aidan cried, "They caught me off guard. We have nothing to hide, so I let them in. They poked around for two hours. I don't think they found anything, but they wouldn't say. Do I need a lawyer?"

"Did they call you a suspect?"

"No, they were respectful to me, but Izzy's got everybody going in all directions. There's no dungeon in the basement, is there?"

Nicholas said, "There's a crypt where Father and our ancestors are buried. As far as anything else, I don't think so. Ask Malcolm. He'll know for sure."

Aidan said he'd call the solicitor in the morning, and Nicholas said that he'd be calling his too. "Stay strong, brother. We did nothing wrong. All this is made up, and she can't prove anything."

"I agree, but she's also talking about the gold. It's going to raise a fuss..."

"It's not, Aidan, because we're in the clear on that too. The gold is in a vault in Glasgow, the tax authorities know all about it, and we've hidden nothing except..." He almost mentioned the gold Carly brought back to America, but thought better of it. If they were asked to turn over their phones, he wanted nothing that would raise eyebrows.

"Let's stop right there for now," Nicholas said. "Tomorrow morning, drive to Mallaig and buy a prepaid cellphone. Call this number —" he looked up the direct line of Sal Broomfield, his attorney "— and leave your number with his assistant. I'll call you back once you've done that."

"Jesus, Nicky. You're scaring me. Is all this about to erupt?"

"Yes, but on your crazy girlfriend, not on us. For now, we have to be careful."

CHAPTER THIRTY-NINE

The local New York stations led off with the sensational story, and Nicholas's daughters were mortified.

"Sexual assault? God, Dad, how can I go back to school when my father's —"

Carly interrupted. "Your father's *what*, Steph? You were there. Your father did nothing to that lunatic. Neither did Aidan. She's nuts and we all know it. Of all people, we three — his family — know Nicky's innocent. I'm ashamed of you. Stand up for your father. Tell your friends Izzy's a nutcase and your dad's a good guy. After that, drop it. This will be old news by the time Christmas break's over anyway."

Nicholas turned up the news, watching as Isabella sat next to her attorney and answered questions. He was glad to watch a few reporters ignore the sensationalism and go after her veracity.

"What proof can you provide that the alleged assault occurred?"

Everything happened just like I said. Get off my back. I've been through a horrible ordeal...

"Has a doctor examined you?"

No. There was too much time between when they let me leave Scotland and when I got here. It's too late now, I guess.

"Will you submit to a polygraph examination?"

Her lawyer put his hand lightly on her arm and took over. "Miss Watson will do whatever it takes to bring Nicholas Dayne and his brother — her common-law husband — to justice. There is also the matter of a fortune in gold. We plan to ensure Miss Watson gets everything that she deserves, despite the family's intent to keep it from her and her husband. Miss Watson personally observed Nicholas Dayne fill a bucket with gold coins — a million dollars' worth, Mr. Dayne told them — and carry it into the castle. It never came out again. The family split it up for themselves, according to Miss Watson, hiding it from the tax authorities and the government. We will ensure Nicholas Dayne and his family are charged with theft of a national treasure."

Izzy sat with a satisfied smirk while the lawyer — whom Carly dubbed a scumbag — tossed out more innuendos, half-truths and blatant lies.

Nicholas opted to call his attorney tonight instead of waiting. Sal wasn't surprised to hear from him, and he suggested a conference call in the morning with Aidan.

But Nicholas had other ideas. "I'll be at your office at ten. I've done nothing wrong, and I don't want to discuss anything on the phone."

The next morning he called downstairs to the doorman and learned there were only two people with cameras out front. Nicholas called his driver, and soon the sedan sat around the corner, ready to make the turn and pick him up.

He caught the reporters off guard. They shouted as Nicholas darted from the building across the sidewalk and into the car's back seat, but their cameras weren't ready, so there were no pictures. At his destination, the Park Avenue building where his company was located had an underground garage, and the driver dropped him at the elevators undisturbed.

His employees glanced up and averted their eyes as he walked through the cavernous trading floor. His assistant welcomed him back, such as it was, and asked if he'd like to arrange a security escort. There was a firm they used occasionally, not so much for protection as to ease his movements through crowds, and he said yes, for the moment that would be a good idea.

The lawyer's office was thirty floors down in his building, and no one spoke to him as he took the elevator. Broomfield's assistant escorted him in, and Sal handed him a slip of paper. "Aidan's number," he said, and asked if he wanted to call now.

"Yes, but I want to speak to him alone," Nicholas said as he put a locked bank bag on the lawyer's desk. "Keep this in your safe for me."

"What is it?"

"Don't ask. Nothing to be concerned about. Keep it for me a few days."

Sitting in a conference room, Nicholas called his half-brother. It was late afternoon in Scotland, and Aidan said he had spoken to his solicitor, who would contact the police and tell them all about the gold. "There's just one problem," Aidan continued. "That sack of coins that fell apart — they put all the coins in a bucket, and you took it to the castle. Those are the coins Noelle and Carly ended up with, right?"

"Right."

"The police in Mallaig want to know where those coins are. Our solicitor told them all the bags were in the bank vault, but Izzy's spouting off about a million dollars in gold coins in a rusty bucket. Now the cops are aggressive, and they intend to come and search again tomorrow. What do I do, Nicky?"

"Everything's good, Aidan. This is why I wanted a secure phone line. There's something I didn't tell you. Remember when the guards drove the pickup filled with bags of gold up to the castle? I supervised the transfer and counted each bag they put into the armored car. Do you remember my doing that?"

He did, and Nicholas continued. "There were millions of dollars in gold. I knew the government would get involved, claims would be asserted, taxes levied, and although the chances our family would get its rightful share are good, it will take months or years until it happens.

"I had decided to split the loose coins. As I told you earlier, I gave Noelle a fourth and Carly the rest. I brought those coins to my lawyer's office this morning, and he'll keep them in a vault until I can get them converted into dollars and distributed.

"I made one more unilateral decision to create a rainy-day fund for the Dayne clan. When I counted the bags going into the armored vehicle, there were forty-three. Those are sitting in the Glasgow bank vault today."

Aidan said, "I'm not sure what you're saying. There were forty-five, and one broke, right?"

"Yes, and only the family knows that. No one else counted the bags as they came out, because everyone was too excited about the loose coins and what they had discovered. The base of the statue held forty-five bags. One ripped, leaving forty-four. While they were transferring the bags from the pickup, I hid one under the tarp. Forty-three went to Glasgow, and the remaining one is in the castle."

"How did you pull it off?"

"Everyone was inside when the armored truck left. I stuck the last bag in the shrubbery by the front door, returned the pickup to the village alone, and walked back to the castle. That night I sneaked down, retrieved the sack, and hid it. I chose not to tell you so you couldn't be blamed if something bad happened. It was my decision, and if you needed it, I would have told you. Looks like now's the time."

"I don't understand how those coins can help our situation."

"Dump the gold from that sack into the old bucket and show it to the police. Tell them here's the gold Izzy says we stole. It's all accounted for, as are all the other bags, as far as anyone knows. We lose our rainy-day fund — at least for the time being — but I have plenty of money to cover any unexpected expenses at the castle."

When he told Aidan where he'd hidden the bag, his brother understood why the policemen didn't come across it when they searched. The closet in Nicky's childhood bedroom had a cleverly concealed false wall on one side that no one would ever notice. He'd found it long ago, and it was where he'd kept his stash of *Playboy* magazines during his teens.

The officers arrived the next day to find a bucket of gold coins waiting for them in the hallway. Aidan apologized that he didn't know yesterday where his brother had hidden them for safekeeping. If the cops had a court order to seize the coins, here they were.

The bucket created a dilemma for the small-town officers. They hadn't been told to confiscate the gold, only to find the missing coins Izzy had described. The police chief refused to assume responsibility for a million dollars in gold, so they left the bucket at Torcall Castle. For the moment, the Dayne clan still had its rainy-day fund.

CHAPTER FORTY

New Year's Eve — December 31

Isabella Watson's sensational story died faster than Carly had predicted. Izzy agreed to a polygraph examination, but when her attorney explained how the procedure would work and what kind of questions she could expect, she changed her mind and refused. Her attorney, who had taken her case on a fifty-fifty contingency after hearing about millions in gold to which she claimed she and her husband were entitled, grilled her about her change of heart.

An hour later, at eleven a.m., he withdrew as counsel, telling the media that certain things had surfaced that made it impossible for him to continue representing Miss Watson.

Nicholas's lawyer pounced on the unusual announcement, and by five o'clock he called with good but not totally unexpected news, given the woman's blatant lies.

Isabella Watson's last name was actually Baker, she was thirty-three, not twenty-four, and she had recently been released from the California Institution for Women in Corona, California. She'd served four years for her third felony offense, this one for defrauding an elderly couple in Palm Springs while acting as their caregiver. Before that, she'd served three years for cashing fifty thousand dollars in checks she stole from her employer, and at the tender age of twenty, she'd spent thirteen months in the Los Angeles County Jail for possession of stolen property.

Izzy had gone to New Mexico to start a new life, or a new criminal enterprise, and she'd had the good fortune of meeting a penniless man who turned out to be heir to a fortune. A would-be con artist who wasn't very good at her work, she tried to pull off one more job, but the resulting publicity ensnared her so quickly, she never really got started.

The lawyer suggested Nicholas and Aidan sue her for defamation of character, but Nicholas disagreed. Why add more publicity to something the world now saw as a feeble attempt at extortion? Isabella was surely gone by now, off to another place and another life and perhaps another con.

On New Year's Eves in the past, Nicholas and Carly would have dressed up and gone dining and dancing with friends. They would have moved from cocktails at the 21 Club to dinner at Jean-Georges or Daniel, and dancing until the wee hours at the Rainbow Room. Tonight would be different, because they were exhausted.

Nine days had passed since the family sat in the first-class lounge at JFK on their way home for Christmas. Nine days that seemed like an eternity, and now at last things were going to settle down. At fifteen minutes until seven on New Year's night, Nicholas, Carly and the girls gathered on the couch in front of his laptop and placed a FaceTime call to Aidan.

At Torcall Castle, it was fifteen minutes to midnight, a quarter of an hour until the moment their father Geoffrey Dayne died ten years ago. If Aidan hadn't become the ninth Earl of Torcall, an ancient curse might have brought down the clan and the castle. At least that was old Uncle Malcolm's assertion.

As they made the connection across the pond, they saw Aidan and Malcolm in the great room. They had moved their chairs together for the call, and the crackling fire behind them stirred Nicholas's memories of how many decisions they had made in that very spot.

Aidan turned away for a moment, and then Laris and John moved into sight behind their chairs. As the clock in Torcall Village rang out the stroke of midnight, everyone raised snifters containing the laird's fine brandy. From a skyscraper in New York City to a remote castle in western Scotland, the words of Malcolm's toast resounded.

The Dayne clan has been ever faithful to the cause of independence. Should it be God's will, let it happen even today. God bless the Dayne family, God bless the laird, and God bless Scotland.

The last chime ended. Twelve times it had rung, and now began the first minute of a new year.

"All's well here," Aidan said, grinning as he clinked glasses with the others. "God bless us indeed!"

CHAPTER FORTY-ONE

Six months later

By June, most of the logistics regarding the treasure cache had been settled. Some documents remained to be signed, but everything was agreed among the Dayne family, the National Museum, Revenue Scotland, and customs, which would rule on if the hoard could leave the country.

Valuation came first. Well-respected numismatists from Edinburgh and London joined forces with a historian from the museum. They met in an underground conference room at the bank where the gold resided, and over five days they opened each sack, cataloged every coin, and agreed on a value that considered all aspects of the unique find. They valued the hoard at seventy million pounds sterling, or about ninety million US dollars, in the coin market.

Next, the lawyers and accountants argued for an adjustment based on what the coins would reasonably bring in a sale. If over eighty thousand Louis d'or coins hit the market at one time, the excess supply would drive down the numismatic value. At last everyone agreed to base the value on the spot price of gold per ounce, which meant the value of the eighty-eight thousand coins was somewhere around forty-five million dollars. Only the family knew about two thousand more coins the Dayne siblings already had.

The museum's proposal required the least negotiation. Considering the prohibitive annual cost of security for something of such value, the curator made what Nicholas considered a reasonable request. He asked for the old bucket, one of the burlap sacks that held the gold, photos of the base being opened, and a hundred gold coins, which were worth forty-four thousand dollars. He intended to create a permanent display as part of their Jacobite section. In exchange, the tax authorities would reduce the family's bill by the amount of the donation.

Customs officials had concerns about two things — the national heritage aspect, which meant allowing the museum as many coins as it wanted, and how to collect taxes on the remainder if it was turned over to the family. At last customs agreed to accept four million pounds as duties, which Nicholas would pay if he could reach an agreement with the tax authorities.

The tax man Cecil Harkins and his aide met by Zoom conference several times with Nicholas and the family's advisors. Two more times in six months Nicholas flew to Edinburgh and met in person, once when negotiations bogged down and then for final negotiations.

Nicholas refused to pay taxes up front on the current price of gold, because that number fluctuated every day. A precipitous drop in gold prices would mean he was paying tax on an inflated number. Instead, he suggested they agree on a percentage of tax due, and he would report and pay taxes each time he sold some of the coins.

Harkins demanded ten percent of the gold be escrowed in the Glasgow vault until the final tax payment was made. Nicholas made a show of protesting, but in reality, it was a reasonable demand, and he used his reluctance as a ploy to get other concessions.

By June, the museum had their exhibit, half of the coins had been sold and Nicholas had paid the customs bill and taxes on twenty-six million dollars from the sale. None of the coins was sold in the open market — they were snapped up by coin dealers around the world. After expenses, each of the four Dayne children had just under five million dollars so far, with at least that much more to come. As residents of the UK, Aidan and Noelle owed no further taxes. Nicholas and Tiona would spend years fighting with the IRS over what they owed. Ultimately it was a few million dollars, leaving each with over eight million dollars in their pockets.

Nicholas made good on his wish to see the family more often. Tiona, who had a new apartment on Columbus Avenue west of Central Park, a new job as assistant director of a nonprofit, and a life free from Xanax, met Nicky and Carly often for dinner.

On his frequent trips to London, Nicholas always saw Noelle, who had dumped Ian, moved into a flat in the West End, and spent some money upgrading her pub and restaurant. Now the Goose & Gander was on the trendy hotspot list of late-night places to go, and she was making money and having fun. Her daughter, Poppy, the black-sheep pole dancer, kept her old job. Better make money while my body's young, she had told her mother, who didn't argue.

He and Aidan spoke by phone several times a week as Nicholas guided him through the machinations of running the estate. He was a quick learner, and the new couple he hired to work with Laris and John had settled in well. They managed the Torcall Castle Bed & Breakfast, Inverness-shire's newest destination resort on the craggy Scottish coast.

Aidan reported Malcolm didn't appear as much these days, preferring not to materialize in front of tourists. He maintained his sense of humor, waiting until a tipsy guest finished his nightcap and walked down the long, dark hall to his bedroom. Malcolm would appear at the far end, wearing his kilt and tam, and scare the pants off the visitor. It made for spooky tales, increased bookings, and the B&B was a profitable venture even from the outset.

Benevolence, Mrs. Campbell, Cook, and Barclay were never seen again. Presumably their work was done now that the ninth Earl of Torcall occupied the castle. Rumors flew about Torcall Village concerning Lord Dayne's new lady friend, that pretty girl Ella from the Sweet Shop in the high street. They'd met that first morning Aidan returned to the castle, the villagers whispered, and of late they'd been seen together often. Perhaps there will be wee ones in their future, they gossiped. And perhaps the Dayne clan will continue to thrive after all.

Thank you!
Thanks for reading *The Last Christmas.*

If you enjoyed it, I'd appreciate a review on Amazon.
Reviews are what allow other readers to find books they
enjoy, so thanks in advance for your help.

Please join me on:
Facebook
http://on.fb.me/187NRRP
Twitter
@BThompsonBooks

If you enjoy a good ghostly thriller,
check out my series called The Bayou Hauntings.

MAY WE OFFER YOU A FREE BOOK?
Bill Thompson's award-winning first novel,
The Bethlehem Scroll, can be yours free.
Just go to
billthompsonbooks.com
and click
"Subscribe."
Once you're on the list, you'll receive advance
notice of future book releases and our newsletter.